Gravely Mistaken

its amazing we've survived!

Gravely Mistaken

Tales of Medicine, Mishaps &
Body Snatching in Augusta, Georgia

Janis Ann Parks

Book Design by Daniel R. Pearson
Cover Photography by Haley and Daryl Reid
www.handdphoto.com

ISBN 1449978800
EAN-13 9781449978808

Printed in the United States

This book is dedicated to Augusta, Georgia
A Southern City of Medicine

Table of Contents

Chapters		Page

ACKNOWLEDGEMENTS

Thanks to and for all my supporters. Lots of gratitude goes to my husband for his encouragement. Thanks also to my daughters for believing in me. Recognition is sent to my friends Celia, Marilyn and Robert for their support. Words of special appreciation go to Paula for her positive comments over the course of years about my writing. Credit goes to Linda for her editorial and encouraging comments. Appreciation also to: Ross, Nancy, Ginger, Ed, Louise, Tom, Steve and members of our former monthly fiction group for their input. A special acknowledgement is extended to Mike, Cleve and Zettie for their perspectives.

A big note of gratitude for extensive editing assistance, graphic design expertise, formatting and set-up goes to Daniel Pearson, publisher of *The Augusta Medical Examiner*.

Also, appreciation to Haley and Daryl of HandD Photography for their enthusiasm and creativity in the course of making the book's cover.

PROLOGUE

A mound of newly sculptured dirt betrayed the location. Cloaked in black to blend in with the secrecy of the night sky, the wagoner halted his horse, and despite his big-boned frame, nimbly jumped down and reached for his digging tools. He moved a small bunch of yellow marigolds aside as if it was delicate crystal.

Directing the shovel with a forceful downward thrust, he located both top corners of the pine box and uncovered enough soil to direct the strike. Switching tools, he wielded the ax, like so many times, smashing and scraping to pull back the top half of the coffin and remove the grisly contents. He had been taught to place a rope around the neck and yank, but finding that distasteful, he had perfected his own technique of straddling the box and grabbing up under the armpits. Lightweights were easy to pull, with one long drag birthing from their burial place head first, but tonight's catch was heavy and required robust tugs with multiple jerking starts and stops. Struggling like a big marlin on a line, it seemed as though he was still alive and thrashing to stay undisturbed in an earthy sea of rest. It was an exhausting tussle, but the wrestler won. With the body beyond rigor mortis, he bound wrists to ankles and stuffed the bent corpse, still clad in his burial shroud, into an oversized burlap sack.

Signaling late autumn, a steamy silver haze clung to midair and spread out in all directions, like a blanket with fingers, as it rose up from the nearby Savannah River with its canal flowing in parallel syncopation. Cedar Grove Cemetery, barely a mile away, began wrapping itself in the humid mist. The poacher knew this forty acre plot of land as well as he knew his job. It had been allotted by the city of Augusta in 1820 as a final resting place for slaves and free blacks. It was where he fished for bodies.

Placing the tools and weighty cargo in the back of the wagon, he chose to finish the cover-up later. Knowing there were still hours of darkness left and no real threat of discovery, he would quench his own thirst while he completed his other chore of collecting whiskey to preserve the cadavers for the anatomy lab.

Hare   Burke

Chapter 1

Burking

Augusta, 1854

Sterling Adams, John Wilkinson Jr., and Owen Dunlop, first-year medical students sitting in Mrs. Gardner's boarding house study room, took time out to rest their lamplight-strained eyes away from their books.

Bamboo shoot thin, with yellow strands of hair topping a boyish and naive looking face, Sterling was curious about his colleagues' opinion. "What do you think of Miss Lucy Clark?"

"Doctor Clark's daughter?" asked John.

"Yes, don't you think she's just the most beautiful...?"

"She is a stunning woman," added Owen.

"I'd like to ask her to the holiday social, but I'm not sure..." Sterling straightened his bow-knotted black silk cravat and smoothed his matching satin vest down to its pockets. Congeniality from his southern plantation upbringing often manifested as indecisiveness and innocence as well as impeccable manners. Cotton was the family estate's main crop, the "King of the South." The puffy white plants dotted nearly all four hundred acres, except for the plots designated for growing cooking vegetables. It was thirty miles across the Savannah toward Charleston, but still in the piedmont and too far west to grow low country rice.

Sterling loved the month of June in South Carolina when sweet corn and tomatoes ripened in the garden. The youngest of seven children born to George and Julia Sterling Adams, he knew he'd be last to inherit the land. He rejoiced on that day, during his twelfth year, when his future avocation fell out of a tree and into his lap. In doctoring the tiny baby squirrel, he discovered his love of helping and healing. He declared that he would dedicate his life tending to the sick. His parents were proud. That was before he knew how much studying it would require.

John playfully winked at his friend. "You might as well go on and ask. The worst she can say is no. And then you'll have your answer. I was thinking of asking a lovely young lady, but I'm afraid she'd be viewed as being beneath our station."

Sterling shot John a querying glance.

John's wide shoulder girth contrasted with his narrowly set blue eyes that peeked out from under a bush of ebony hair. He was two years older than his classmates with immeasurably more sophistication and maturity, except for his love of pranks. The son of a Philadelphia lawyer, he was strongly encouraged to pursue the medical profession by his father, a skilled prosecutor. Both John Wilkinson, Sr. and Doctor Benjamin Williams, the physician who'd attended his difficult birth and mother's subsequent death, presented becoming a physician as some sort of atonement, which the young man accepted.

Doctor Williams had even arranged an apprenticeship with Doctor Dugas, a fellow graduate from their 1829 class at the University of Maryland. John found his previous years' experience with Dugas in Augusta both stimulating and rewarding.

Owen chimed in with his burly Scotsman manner. Ancestral streaks of auburn blazed in his goatee, "I wouldn't be caught dead escorting a female to the social. Not that I don't like women, mind you, but our professors might not think I was completely serious about my studies. Besides, isn't it a stuffy parlor gathering?"

"Right..." Sterling's enthusiasm dwindled. "Maybe I'll put off thinking about it until next week. There's so much studying to do now, memorizing all those bones and muscles." He groaned and slumped against the back of his chair. "Our anatomy class is about to kill me. Or at least the smell might. How many times do we have to watch a dissection? I'm not at all interested in surgery and I'm having a difficult time distinguishing tendons and ligaments. I only wanted to be a country doctor. Why do I have to learn all those bones and muscles?"

"What a lot of griping, Sterling. You better not let Doc Campbell hear you say any of that, or he'll make our exams even harder. Next year we'll be expected to do the cadaver slicing. "

"Where do you suppose our anatomy subjects come from?" Sterling seemed surprised at his own question.

"I once thought stories about unearthing cadavers to obtain subjects for medical schools were rubbish." John mused and rubbed his right index finger over his chin, "but I remember my father talking about body snatching scandals back in Philadelphia. I've heard that some of the Northern cemeteries look like battlefields in spring when the snows thaw because of all the grave digging. There was some sort of public address by a Doctor Shippen who refuted the accusations, but…"

"Really?" Sterling acted shocked.

"Well, there has to be some way for us to learn our anatomy lessons. Some medical students in England had to dig up their own specimens for classes. At least we don't have to do that," Owen sighed with relief.

"What do they call those unfortunates who are tasked with digging up the dead?" John wondered.

"Sack-em-up gentlemen or Resurrectionists."

"Owen, you know a lot about the *'old country'*. What about those famous grave robbers in Scotland?" John's voice inflected a growing sense of excitement.

Owen responded in his most serious scholarly voice as he cleared his throat, "Burke and Hare, Edinburgh, eighteen-twenty-eight. Confessed to providing sixteen bodies to the anatomists at the medical school, but thought to have murdered as many as thirty people." Then in a more relaxed manner he added, "But they weren't exactly grave robbers."

John egged him on. "Keep going, Owen. You're such a good storyteller. Spin us a yarn with what you know about them."

"Well, my family was from Edinburgh before they came to this country in the early thirties, so I have heard quite a bit about them. Burke and Hare were actually Irishmen who came to Scotland to work on building the Union Canal, which was constructed between eighteen-eighteen and eighteen-twenty-two. There is no evidence that they knew each other then, though. They met up years later. Nefarious creatures, they were."

The study room was on the second floor to the right of the top of the stairs. A corner fireplace provided heat and three whale oil lamps with their small round wick tubes gave light. Sitting open on the long rectangular oak table was a copy of Cutter's *Anatomy Physiology and Hygiene* with its one hundred and fifty engravings. The young men prepared for their lessons by quizzing each other on body parts, but John and Sterling were eager to continue this current interruption. They moved their straight-backed chairs away from the table and closer to Owen to give him center stage as he went on.

"William Hare found lodgings in a boarding house in the West Port area of Edinburgh and eventually took up with the widow woman who ran it named Margaret Laird. They began living as common-law man and wife and ran the house together. He was said to be a 'ghastly reptilian looking sort of man' with sunken cheeks and a long nose. Also, he supposedly had a sinister laugh. William Burke was older than Hare, but he was reported to have softer features with a younger, kinder look. He had a wife and children back in Ireland, but the family never joined him in Scotland. He became enamored of a Scots woman named Helen McDougal and after the canal work was complete they moved off together. Traveling about and performing all manner of odd jobs to make money, the pair did everything, from working on farms to mending shoes. They eventually came to West Port as well and one day Maggie met Helen at the market. They struck up an instant friendship. She invited them over to the boarding house to have the men meet and not long after they became paying lodgers. The four of them shared a love of drink and a penchant for making easy money, but they fought fiercely as well."

"How did they start stealing bodies?" John was anxious to get to the gruesome part of the tale.

"Hold on. Do you want to hear the entire story?"

"Oh, yes please, I'll be quiet."

"Good, then sit back and relax. So, picture this. One day in November eighteen-twenty-seven, the twenty-ninth, I believe it was, an old Army pensioner named

Donald, who was boarding with them, up and died of the dropsy. You know, too much fluid in the lungs; heart failure. It seems that Donald died before he'd paid his monthly rent of four pounds. William Hare was furious. He went into a sort of tirade about being cheated. Burke was consulted and the two cooked up a scheme to replace Donald's body in the coffin with an equal weight of tree bark. A solemn funeral service was held over the deception, the whole while the old man's body lay in another room under a bed. After the coffin was taken away, Burke and Hare carried a sack containing Donald's remains over to the Surgeon's Square where they were directed to the lecture rooms of the Anatomist, Robert Knox. Doctor Knox's assistants paid seven pounds ten shillings for poor old Donald, given that his body was so fresh and they also gave a hint that more bodies would be welcome."

Sterling was wide-eyed, "Seven pounds, if I'm calculating correctly, that was almost two month's lodging."

"Right you are. It seemed a small fortune and they were so impressed with the easy money, they began to look for other ways to acquire bodies. Not long after Donald's death, another boarder named Joseph the miller took sick. He wasn't failing quite quickly enough to suit Burke and Hare's fancy and they were afraid that his fever might be scaring off other lodgers, so they thought to help him on his way and end his suffering. Whiskey was poured for Joseph until he was so drunk that he passed out. Burke held his nose and mouth shut whilst Hare straddled across his body and restrained him tightly until he suffocated. This became their modus operandi. Fresh corpses with no marks made perfect specimens for anatomy students."

Owen, thrilled to have such a captive audience, leaned

into the circle, his eyes ablaze with excitement and reflection of the firelight.

"When they ran out of sickly lodgers, they moved on to elderly prostitutes and vagrants. Burke and Hare were fetching up to ten pounds per body and they didn't have to expend the physical work of digging up graves. They thought they had figured out the perfect scheme, but they began to get cocky and careless. Their tenth victim was a prostitute by the name of Mary Paterson who was especially well known and supposedly recognized by several of Doctor Knox's students."

"How do you suppose those students knew her?" Sterling's naïveté made John shake his head and cluck.

Sterling tried to defend himself, "Well, I'm just trying to understand the story."

Owen reached over and touched Sterling's forearm, "You know, they were intimately familiar with her."

"Oh…"

"Keep going," John insisted.

"Mary was supposed to have been quite beautiful, voluptuous. Her body was preserved in whiskey for three months at Surgeon's Square so that it could be studied and admired. Artists even came with their sketchpads. Could it have been obsession and erotic interest in the dead, perhaps? After a while, two of Doctor Knox's assistants began to suspect how her corpse had been acquired. Burke and Helen moved into their own lodging house sometime in the summer because of some falling out with the Hares, but the two murdering men continued their teamwork. When they killed Daft Jamie, they caused quite a stir."

"What is a Daft Jamie?" asked Sterling.

Owen put his index finger up to the side of his head and traced circles. "He was, well you know, not quite right in the head. He also walked with a limp because of a clubfoot. His real name was James Wilson, a fairly well known riddler and entertainer of children in the neighborhood. Their usual method for demise had to be altered since Jamie was only eighteen years old and he refused to drink enough whiskey to pass out. He eventually did doze off on one of the spare beds in the boarding house, but when Burke tried to smother him, there was a fierce fight. Burke and Hare finally did overcome him though and he also landed on the anatomy table. Jamie was quite recognizable because of that foot of his. Doctor Knox vehemently denied his identity and went to work immediately cutting up those obvious bits. You see, the dissections in Surgeons' Square were open to the public. Sometimes as many as five hundred people, mostly aspiring medical students, would attend."

"Really? It seems so secretive here." John interjected.

"Oh, I agree. Here in the Colonies, it's more clandestine. It's not so in Scotland. Doctor Knox was a famous and popular anatomist, at least in those days. He was said to have a flamboyant style, giving brilliant, expert lectures. Students attending his course were guaranteed to see the human body completely dissected."

Sterling interrupted, "Is that the same Robert Knox that wrote *The Races of Men*?"

"Yes, he is the very same. Doctor Campbell mentioned him in class just the other day, remember? His treatise is that race is everything. Literature, science, art; all of civilization depends on it. He certainly believes that the anatomies of Negroes and Caucasians differ greatly."

"Maybe he should move to the South," John suggested sarcastically.

Owen continued with his story, "But the murder that was Burke and Hare's undoing was Mary Docherty. Burke was in a tavern on Halloween morning, eighteen-twenty-eight. He struck up a conversation with the old Irish woman and after finding out that she was, coincidentally, from the same small town as his mother, he convinced her that they must be related. He took her back to his boarding house where she stayed for dinner and more drink. Ann and James Gray, another pair of boarders, were shipped off to Hare's house in order to make room for Mary. The Grays returned for breakfast in the morning and found Mary gone. Helen McDougal claimed she sent the old woman packing because during the night she had become way too friendly with her lover. But when Ann Gray went to the spare room to search for a lost stocking, Burke became so adamant about her staying away from the bed, that her suspicions were aroused. Later when she was able to sneak back to the bedroom, undetected, Ann caught a glimpse of the woman's body hidden under straw beneath the bed. Appalled, the Grays left the house to alert the authorities, but not before Helen offered them a bribe to keep quiet. When the police started questioning, they heard differing versions of the same stories."

"Were they all convicted?' Sterling asked, still wide-eyed.

"No, now the story takes a strange twist. The Hares were offered a King's pardon immunity to testify against Burke and Helen, which they did. Helen got off as 'not proven,' but Burke was convicted and sentenced to hang. He made a complete confession. Doctor Knox was never indicted, but his anatomy demonstrations became quite unpopular. There was a public execution in January, eighteen-twenty-nine, with a huge crowd in attendance. They yelled for Hare and Knox to be hanged as well, but they settled to see Burke drop. Ironically, Burke's body was turned over to number ten Surgeons' Square for dissection. There was so much clamoring to view his dismemberment; Burke's body was placed on display for two days, partially dissected, with an estimated forty thousand people who filed past. Supposedly some lucky folks got to keep some of his skin as a souvenir. His skeleton remains at Edinburgh University. There was even a ballad written about them:

> *Up the close and down the stair,*
> *In the house with Burke and Hare*
> *Burke's the butcher, Hare's the thief,*
> *Knox, the boy who buys the beef.*

> *Burke and Hare,*
> *Fell down the stair,*
> *With a body in a box,*
> *Going to Doctor Knox.*

"What a story," John had hung on to Owen's every word.

"Fear of murder for dissection became the subject of mass public hysteria. It was called Burking Mania or Burkophobia. Newspapers reported attempted burkings. This was actually the origin of the word 'burking' which means to kill for the sake of obtaining a body." Owen still held their attention. "London gained its own set of burkers, Bishop and Williams. They had been grave robbers, but they progressed to drowning their victims in a garden well."

"Do you suppose there is burking going on here in Augusta?" John asked.

"I doubt that, but I wouldn't be surprised if some of our specimens weren't the handiwork of a resurrectionist."

"Remember, a resurrectionist is someone who digs up bodies" John glanced at Sterling preemptively.

"I think I could use a drink, now," Sterling added.

"Hang on, Sterling. Do you really think so, Owen?"

"Haven't you wondered about the porter who works down in the anatomy lab, Harris something or other? I've heard his nickname is the 'Resurrection Man,'" Owen spoke with his almost imperceptible brogue.

John piped up, "Yes, well, I'm certainly wondering about it now. I hadn't heard his nickname, but the more I hear about the whole subject of body snatching and taking into account the fact that dissection is illegal, there could be some sort of market for bodies. Maybe not freshly murdered ones, but certainly freshly buried ones."

Sterling added, "We had more than twenty slaves working on our plantation in South Carolina and I remember hearing that they have different ideas about the dead... kind of skittish about them...strange beliefs about spirits and all. I just don't know if I believe that a darkie could be a resurrectionist. Going into a graveyard at night? It gives me the shivers."

"Sterling, what choice does a slave have except to do his master's bidding?" John added, "I believe we use the impoverished, inferior members of our society as specimens because their protests would never be heard. And even if their anatomy is somewhat different from ours...well, what I mean to say is...have you noticed that most of our cadavers are Negroes?"

Owen continued the thread, "Criminals, debtors... there was mortification among the destitute. No pun intended. Besides public humiliation, the apprehension of dissection was that they might be slit before they were really dead. And in the cemeteries, which are called Kirk yards in Scotland, guards were placed on patrol and families were applying mort-safes to graves. The Anatomy Act was passed in Britain in eighteen-thirty-two legalizing dissection as an attempt to end burking and bodysnatching."

"What is a mort-safe?" It was Sterling again.

"It's a collection of iron bars that fit over the top of a gravesite. It's designed to make it much more difficult to dig it up. Resurrectionists are only willing to do so much hard work to steal a body. The mort-safe had to stay put just until the cadaver was too decomposed to be useful to an anatomist."

"Oh," Sterling gazed seriously at his friend, "so, John, are you thinking that it might be true that the porter is a grave robber?"

"It is a fascinating thought, don't you think?"

"I find the idea of going down to the tavern for a slosh to calm my nerves fascinating. Isn't anyone else interested in that?" Sterling persisted.

"Listen chaps; I promised Mrs. Gardner some assistance with her spinning wheel. I used to help my mother with hers and when I mentioned that, well now I fear she thinks I'm expert. But I told her I'd see what I can do to help and it's getting late," Owen declined.

"All right, Owen, while you assist our lovely landlady, please impart to her that we may be out late tonight. We'll drink an extra pint for you." John waved toward Owen as he replaced his chair and exited the room.

Sterling was following close behind as he said, "See you later, Owen. Thanks for the education and entertainment."

"Certainly, it was my pleasure." Owen made his way down the stairs to the front sitting room.

Chapter 2

Spinning Wheels

Amanda Gardner sat on a stool next to her spinning wheel facing the parlor entrance. Thirty-three years old and brunette with brown eyes like the center of a sunflower, her disposition was anything but cheery. Owen thought of her as melancholy, but she wore the style of the day to create the tiny waist deception and he thought her tight corseting might also affect her disposition. He considered it one of his first medical opinions.

The two scalawags heading for the tavern donned their outer coats and gloves and made a dash to the front door. "Good night, Mrs. Gardner, Owen. We'll see your 'fixed spinner' work tomorrow."

"John and Sterling wanted me to tell you that they may be out quite late tonight." Owen deliberately projected his voice toward the door, within earshot of the two, so they were assured their request had been fulfilled.

Amanda had a special affinity for medical students as

she had once been married to a physician, Paul Gardner. One year after their nuptials, at the age of eighteen, her thoughts of wedded bliss were short-lived as she found herself widowed. There had been no time for conception. She inherited the three story brick dwelling on the gas-lamp illuminated corner of Greene and McIntosh Streets. Paul's brethren had encouraged her to open the home as a boarding house for students attending the Medical College, which they promised she'd always have filled. Resistant at first and uncomfortable with the idea of surrounding herself with medical memories reminiscent of her marital void, her need for self-sufficiency became undeniable, and she yielded to their suggestion. Discovering that she loved the young men's company, she enjoyed filling her time by tending to their needs and watching their metamorphosis to physicians. The modest, but contemporarily furnished home had already hosted thirty graduates. Amanda recently had a new brown-checkered oilcloth laid over the hallway floor to keep street dirt from spreading through to all the rooms.

Gracie, her cook, gardener, laundry maid and servant had been a wedding gift from her parents. Broom, the butler, had come with Paul and stayed on with her after he died. Broom looked after the horse and her hay, the carriage, firewood and tended to the privy. A red brick stable with two wooden doors housed the horse on the left, carriage on the right and hay was stored in the loft above. Amanda relied heavily on her servants to keep the house running in an orderly manner.

Gracie or Broom could have inspected Amanda's spinning wheel and even possibly worked on it, but neither of them gave her any heat. Amanda felt a fire whenever she found herself close to Owen and it had been a long time since she'd felt that. Even through her tight whalebone undergarment, her bosom felt full and rose up inside her dress as he approached.

"So, what sort of problem do we have here, Mrs. Gardner?" Owen almost bounced into the room.

"I...I'm sorry if I'm keeping you from going off with your friends, Owen." Amanda hesitated and became flustered whenever she tried to talk to him.

"No matter, I'd actually rather stay here and help you."

"Really?" Amanda wanted to believe him, but she had a question in her voice. "I've asked Gracie to make us some tea."

"Tea sounds wonderfully pleasant." Owen plopped down on the divan. Green gingham slipcovers were in place to protect the upholstery from dust and soot. A slate fireplace mantel was painted to mimic fine Italian marble. Burning wood pushed out warmth from the hearth. Placed in symmetric balance at each end of the mantel ledge, two brass candelabras with dangling prisms sprayed extra light around the room.

"What is that wonderful aroma?"

"It could be lavender. Gracie set some to dry last week. I...I dressed the florets with a touch of cinnamon and cloves and put it in that bowl." Amanda pointed to a white china bowl sitting on the marble topped table near the doorway.

Owen hopped up and went over to have a whiff, "Oh, what a lovely smell; some sweetness, but with a little spice, too. It reminds me of you...and of my mother's linens." Owen coaxed Amanda, hoping for a smile. "But, I think the smell I was referring to earlier was food."

"I should have guessed that. You young men are always hungry, aren't you?" A faint hint of relaxation and enjoyment was beginning to show on her face.

Gracie came in with a serving tray loaded with a teapot, two cups, and a plate full of lemon gingerbread squares.

"That was what I smelled. Gracie you've done it again.

You've baked something wonderful."

"Why, Mr. Owen, you don't say? I might blush all up if you keep on." She looked down toward her feet and took an embarrassed little side step.

"Yes, I do say. Gracie, your food is wonderful."
Gracie grabbed the corners of her white apron and curtsied. "Thank you, sir. Will you be needing anything else, Ma'am?"

"No, that will be all Gracie. I will see you in the morning."

Gracie and Broom shared the servants' quarters over the kitchen and laundry rooms. They were off to the left and back of the main house. Gracie's footsteps could be heard moving toward the back door.

Amanda held up the sugar bowl and tilted it toward Owen with an asking gesture.

"No, thank you, I take my tea without."

Owen looked at the teacup and cautiously pulled a flask loaded with Scotch Whiskey out of his vest pocket. He measured Amanda's reaction.

"But with..." he pointed to the flask. "Would you care for a little spike?"

"That might be splendid...not too much, though."
Amanda heard her words, but her emotions conflicted. She wanted more of something else.

Amanda ate one of Gracie's lemon gingerbread squares and looked on while Owen ate the other five. His hunger intrigued her. She wondered if those sweets would really satisfy him. She wanted to devour this man sitting in front of her, Victorian shamefulness aside. It had been years since she'd felt any masculine warmth and she'd wanted to have her way with him, even before the whiskey.

"What made you want to become a doctor, Owen?"

"Brian, my little brother, died in a yellow fever epidemic in Boston. He was only three years old. My father was a canal engineer and came to this country in eighteen-thirty-three along with James Francis. He worked on the Merrimack and other canals in the Boston area. I was born in eighteen-thirty-five and we moved here ten years later."

"So, your father came here to Augusta to work on our canal?"

"Yes, he and Mother stayed here six years. Then they moved on to the Erie, to work on a widening project. They seem to think they'll stay there quite a while."

"My husband, Paul, died in a Yellow Fever epidemic, too."

Owen searched in Amanda's eyes for her truth. "It's a horrible thing to watch someone go through, isn't it?"

"Absolutely gruesome."

"That's why I'm attending medical school. I want to stop gruesomeness."

Amanda was wearing her royal blue dress. The bodice cinched tightly about her waist while the brocaded skirt flared out over multiple petticoats. Pinned at the top of her rounded dress collar was a broach with matching blue stones. A blue and white shawl embraced her shoulders. Her hair was drawn up loosely into a bun with evidence of her natural wave on the sides of her head.

Owen moved over toward the spinning wheel. "So let's discuss what is wrong with this wheel."

"When I sat down to spin yesterday, the treadle seemed to be sticking."

"Show me." Owen had a dictatorial tone to his voice. She wanted to obey. She stood up and moved over to sit at the stool next to the spinning wheel. She moved the flywheel slightly to start it and placed her right foot on the treadle. As soon as she pushed down, the wheel gagged.

Owen diagnosed the problem, "It's practically nothing.

I think it just needs a little oil. Do you have any?"
"Really?" she seemed surprised.
"Well, we could take it all apart and put it back together, if you'd like something more serious to be wrong with it."
Amanda laughed.
"That's what I've been waiting for...a laugh." Owen smiled at her.
"I believe I know where there is an oil can." Amanda got up and walked toward a cabinet in the back hallway. She felt distracted and out of breath. Her thoughts were no longer on the spinning wheel. She hypnotically reentered the room and handed the can to Owen.
He placed a few drops of the lubricant onto junctions at the footman and flywheel. He pressed the treadle with his feet to display the smoothed spinning wheel action. "What do you think? Isn't that ever so much better? Shall we try a bobbin?"
"I'm feeling a little sheepish that this was so simple." Amanda moved over toward Owen, a bobbin in her outstretched hand. She hoped as he took the object from her hand, she would feel his touch. He stood up and moved closer to her. The attraction was beginning to overcome them both. She thought she might swoon. Instead she said, "We'll have something to show the others in the morning."
Owen took the spindle and placed it on the wheel, then turned to Amanda.
"Why don't you sit down and test it?"
She became unable to hold back any longer as she moved closer to him and melted into the space where he was standing. Her mouth rose up to meet his. She felt as though her eyes were looking through netting. The whiskey had added a new layer to her usual state of painlessness.

Owen grabbed Amanda by the elbows and met her lips. He kissed her deeply and began to dance her toward the best room. She floated backward as he steered her forward; their fondling pace increasing. The best room was that closed-door space on the first floor to the left of the stairs reserved for guests, but there had been no guests in the house for years.

• • •

Huddled over a small corner table near a back window at Bristow's tavern John leaned over on his elbow toward Sterling, "I've finally thought of a nickname for you."

"Really? I'm afraid to ask what it might be. Dunce or perhaps like the old Indian name, Slowtocatchon?"

John clicked his tongue, "No, neither one of those. I know you've been sheltered with your family's southern plantation kind of life. It'll take you a while to get as wise and experienced as us northern city folk. Drinking ale and coveting pretty women are good beginnings. No, I was thinking of the nickname Strawling. Firstly, because of your blonde, straw-like hair and secondly because of your Southern speech. How do you drawl your words out like that?"

Sterling distinctly and methodically elongated every word in sarcasm,

"Well, sir, it is all a part of that southern plantation life."

"Absolutely amazing."

"Southerners have had a lot of experience. Give us our due. My grandfather was an inventor of the cotton gin."

"You're related to Eli Whitney?"

"Not really. My grandfather's name was Sebastian Adams. He knew Whitney, though. It's a long story that I'll save for another day when you're more respectful of my drawl."

John laughed, "Alright, I'll be waiting."

Sterling laughed back, "I'll be waiting as well."

They were onto drinking their second round of ale as Sterling stretched his neck, shifted in his seat and pointed out the window, "Oh, look, John."

"It's that scrawny little mill kid I helped Doctor Dugas take care of. He must be headed home after his shift at the factory. Tommy's his name. Tommy Three Fingers. He says he wants to be a doctor someday. I'm not sure there's much hope for that."

"No, not there, look over there," Sterling redirected John's gaze, "Doesn't that resemble our old medical wagon that's usually parked out behind the anatomy building? Look, someone's getting out!"

Peering out of the pub window, they watched as a big shadowy hulk of a man jumped down from his ledge-like seat, tethered his horse to a hitching post and disappeared, slipping into a narrow service doorway at the back of the bar meant for deliveries.

"Sterling, I'll bet that is the porter who works down in the anatomy lab, the one that Owen referred to earlier as a Resurrectionist."

"I remember his name. It's Grandison Harris. Do you think he really is some kind of grave robber?"

"I don't know, but maybe we can find out. Let's go see what he's up to."

John was like a young schoolboy catching a glimpse of his teacher's petticoats and his sense of mischief was growing, but Sterling remained wary.

Both young men paid for their drinks and donned their coats and gloves to go out into the street. Sterling and John made their way around to the back of the brown river-stone tavern. Managing to stay hidden in the alley shadows, they were near enough to the doorway to detect a sweet sticky odor of spilled alcohol mixed with mustiness.

They heard Harris talking, "I needs to be picking up that whiskey you've got ordered for the Docs at the school. But I'll takes another drink first. I gots more work to do tonight. I was up the hill a ways when my wagon wheel needed fixing. That's how come I's so covered with dirt."

John whispered eagerly to Sterling, "It sounds as though he'll linger here a while longer. Let's go see what he's got in the wagon."

Sterling glanced around nervously, "What if he catches us?"

"We'll think of something if that time comes. Besides we practically know him. Come on."

"Alright, but let's be quick about it."

They cautiously made their way over to where the horse was tied.

Peering inside the wagon-box, John motioned, "Psst... Strawling...there's a huge burlap sack full of something in here and it's not potatoes."

Sterling pulled his white linen handkerchief from his coat pocket and dabbed at his runny nose. "Let's hurry, it's cold out here. If it's not a sack of potatoes, do you think it's a body?"

"No thinking about it. Look, this fellow's huge. Help me get him out of here." John tugged at the bulky bag.

"What are you doing?"

"I've got a great idea for a practical joke. Let's take this dead man out of here and stash him somewhere. Then I'll get back in the bag and scare the daylights out of the porter. It'll be a riot. Just as soon as he sets foot in the buggy, I'll moan a little and we'll have some fun." His eyes sparkled with anticipation.

"John, have you gone crazy?"

"Oh, come on, don't be an old stick-in-the-mud. What's wrong with playing a little prank?"

Sterling's voice took on a sarcastic tone, "Well, it doesn't seem so little to me, but I certainly wouldn't want to be the old fogey to spoil your fun."

"Grab these feet and we'll take him down the side alley."

The young men struggled to maneuver the bulky cadaver from the wagon.

"You're right, he's like a whale," Sterling groaned.

"Not quite, and I've got the heaviest part. Come on, let's hurry it up."

Bowed under the weight, they carried the corpse to the closest, darkest spot they could find, tucked the dead man on his side between the brick façade at the rear of the Georgia Railroad Bank building and its metal fire escape, then hurried back to the buckboard.

John peeled off his coat and gloves and pushed them toward his friend. "Here, hold these for me. I'll be back shortly to collect." He leapt in the back of the wagon and picked up the burlap sack.

Sterling stuffed John's gloves in his pockets and threw the coat over his shoulder in preparation for the next command.

"Quick, help me into this bag. Whew, this smells like death. I hope he comes out soon. You hide out of sight somewhere."

"Better you than me if it smells bad. I think I see him coming."

Weaving slightly with a wide gait, the big black porter was carrying a whiskey barrel. He placed the cask close to the sack where John was hiding and went to the post to untie the horse's reins.

Sterling stayed hidden and held his breath as he watched Grandison climb into the wagon and take command. He wondered how long his colleague would wait to play his trick.

Unexpectedly, the roan mare named Bessie kicked back as the reins tightened and the porter lost his grip. The horse had already begun to bolt away and wagon wheels were furiously spinning by the time John's feeble cry came from the bag on the floor of the buckboard.

Sterling called out to his friend, but his voice was drowned out by Harris' pleas for Bessie to whoa and the sound of clomping hooves fleeing on cobblestones.

Chapter 3

Surgery

1812-1832

Mr. B had been suffering with left lower back pain for nearly a week. It came in waves, radiating to the front of his abdomen and then shooting down his left leg. Spasms came like thunderous rumblings threatening to split the ground beneath his feet and lightning sensations coursed back up his spine leaving the agony to lodge behind his eyes. Accompaniments to the colic were nausea, vomiting and sleeplessness.

Moments of relief were wracked with fears of recurrence.

Thoughts of ending the torment by his own hand included jumping off the bridge with bricks tied to his shoes to ensure swallowing by the river or drinking an entire bottle of the opium-laced alcohol remedy he was using to dull his anguish. Visions of his wife and six children stopped him. He had a new appreciation for her endurance if his pain was akin to childbirth.

Mr. B doubled over in his suffering. He could bear it no longer and he had to have it stopped. As his last resort, he presented himself to the local hospital where the physician declared, "Kidney stones, my good man. The only way to relieve them, I'm sorry to say is surgical removal."

A laborer for forty of his fifty-six years, Mr. B saw no other choice but to submit to the knife. He was unable to work in his current state of incapacitation and he was unable to pass the stones of his own volition.

Led to the hospital's dingy-walled room designated for operations, Mr. B was given a triple shot of whiskey laced with poppy juice. With his sensibilities approaching stupor, two assistants bound him in a crouching position to allow access to the cause of his obstruction. His hands were tied to the soles of his feet and his knees touched his shoulders. Lying on his side, the patient was strapped onto the slab of wood that served as an operating table. It had grooved, slanted channels to direct the flow of blood to waiting buckets of sawdust stationed on the floor.

The operation was called a lithotomy, the surgical incision of the urinary bladder for removal of a stone, the most common surgical procedure of the day. The mark of a competent lithotomist's surgical skill was speed. The physician made an incision and began the probing, like a policeman on the trail of a killer.

Mr. B let out sharp, loud cries.

Searching for clues of the calculus' whereabouts, the operator switched between various instruments, thrusting and poking anew with each. Attempting to collar the offender, every investigation penetrated deeper, but the hunted remained elusive.

"Leave the stone in," screamed the victim.

Exasperated, the physician wiped his hands on his apron before reaching into the open cavity with his bare fingers. He finally pulled out the offending calcification with a triumphant sweep.

Mr. B did not share in the celebration, as he had drawn his last breath during the protracted torment.

• • •

Milton Antony had been a witness, sitting toward the back of the crowded surgical theatre, the day Mr. B was splayed open. He was on the brink of beginning his study of medicine. Outrage at the inhuman treatment of the patient and the apparent lack of skill possessed by his surgeon gave Antony cause to abhor the incompetence that contributed to the scandalous reputation of many medical practitioners of his day, especially surgeons.

Antony was a forward-looker. Clean-shaven around the slight dimple in his chin, dark hair swept over to the right and covering his ear on that side, his eyes were set toward the future of medicine. He moved to Augusta, the city on the Savannah River, in 1819 after attending the only session of medical lectures he could afford at the University of Pennsylvania and serving a seven-year preceptorship with a physician in Monticello, Georgia. His passion became organizing, standardizing and educating the future physicians of the world.

A petition to create a Medical Academy, put forth by Antony, was granted by the governor of Georgia in December, 1828. Joining Antony to teach for the first term were his two colleagues, Joseph Adams Eve and Ignatius Poultney Garvin. These three faculty men taught a seven-member student body for a first term lasting from October of 1829 through May of 1830.

"Gentlemen, we have a problem." It was Lewis

DeSaussure Ford speaking as the first dean of the school. The faculty had been called together to discuss a recent correspondence received form the Medical College of South Carolina.

"They will not recognize our students."

"What exactly do you mean?" quizzed Doctor Eve. Antony answered, "Our original concept of a one year academy with credits transferable to another medical school has been rejected. South Carolina indicates it cannot make the desired arrangement until our institution is placed on equal footing with other medical institutions in the country."

Dean Ford rubbed several strands of his long curly beard in between his thumb and forefinger, a habit he enjoyed when he was particularly pensive. The 1822 graduate of the College of Physicians and Surgeons in New York City added, "We will have no credibility unless we are able to graduate our own students. We must apply to the legislature for expansion to two courses of lectures. That will allow us to confer the degree of Doctor of Medicine and legitimize our program."

Joseph Eve had attended his first course of lectures in Liverpool, England, apprenticed in the office of Doctor Antony and graduated in 1828 from the Medical College of South Carolina in Charleston. "If my alma mater won't accept us as a one year academy, no institution will. What steps must we take?"

"I will need to make another trip to Milledgeville to make application to the governor and legislature of this fair state," declared Anthony.

Doctor Garvin, husband to Milton Antony's daughter, agreed.

"So be it," was the consensus in the room.

It was these physicians who represented the core of the early school and were delighted when approval was received from the capitol for its program to lengthen. Another celebration occurred for the newly reorganized Medical Institute in the spring of 1832, when the trustees gave recommendation to increase the faculty to a maximum of six.

Applications from two candidates came before the faculty for review.

Dean Ford read the letters of qualifications. "The first candidate is Doctor Louis Alexander Dugas. Born January third, eighteen-hundred-six in Washington, Wilkes County, he attended the Academy of Richmond County at the age of fifteen. He studied for a time in the office of Doctor Charles Lambert de Beauregard, a French émigré practicing in Augusta from eighteen-twenty to eighteen-twenty-two. When Beauregard died, Dugas continued his studies with Doctor John Dent before entering the medical department at the University of Maryland. After graduating, he spent a year at a family friend's plantation in Georgia, pursuing more independent study and in eighteen-twenty-eight he departed for Europe spending the next three years traveling in England, France, Switzerland, Germany and Italy. Paris served as his headquarters. He attended a full course of lectures at the Sorbonne and attended surgical operations, post-mortem examinations and during hospital rounds he accompanied professors on their visits. He was present during the revolution and saw the first man killed at the Palais Royal."

Antony interrupted, "Did you say anything about his lineage?"

"Let me see, his father was Louis Rene Dugas de Vallon, of French West Indian descent and his mother was also a native of Santo Domingo. It says here that the de Vallon was dropped from their surname when the family immigrated to the United States from Santo Domingo, prior to his birth."

Joseph Eve posed the question, "And what of his surgical skills?"

"He is said to specialize in penetrating wounds of the abdomen. And he has a reputation as an excellent lithotomist. He's certainly had extensive international training."

Ford stroked his long hair, which hung down below the collar of his coat rivaling the length of his beard and looked at Doctor Eve. "And I believe you have personal knowledge of our other candidate, Paul Fitzgerald Eve?"

"That is a fact. His father, Captain Oswell Eve, is the brother of my father, Joseph Eve, making him my first cousin. For that reason I feel that I should, perhaps, disqualify myself from a vote."

"Nonsense, nepotism is nothing to shirk. We now certainly know his lineage."

"In that case I shall attempt to remain as objective as possible."

Dean Ford picked up a second set of papers and began to read. "Paul Fitzsimmons Eve was born June twenty-seventh, eighteen-hundred-six in Forest Hall on the Savannah River near Augusta. He attended Franklin College in Athens, Georgia. Moving to Philadelphia, he attended the University of Pennsylvania and studied under Charles Meigs. The same year he graduated with his Medical Doctorate, eighteen-twenty-eight, he sailed for Europe and while in Paris witnessed the dethronement of Charles X. Getting through to Poland with Lafayette's assistance, he offered his services in the war against Russia. He was assigned to hospital duty and spent thirty days as a prisoner within Prussian lines. Falsely claiming that he had a case of cholera, he was freed and decorated by the Polish Army with the golden cross of honor."

Antony remarked, "Yet another example of extensive

international training . . . impressive. And what of his skills?"

"It is reported that Doctor Eve is able to amputate a limb and bandage the stump in less than two minutes. He is also an excellent lithotomist."

"This would seem to pose as a challenging decision."

Antony spoke up, "I think not. We need to retain them both."

Eve questioned, "Whatever for? It is a reduplication of skills."

"Exactly, it will create competition, a sort of camaraderie with an edge. Think 'promotion of excellence.' They'll spur each other to great heights."

"Brilliant idea," Ford proclaimed. "They are of the same ilk. Not only will they compete with each other for new and innovative treatments, they will force each other to new frontiers."

"I hope the edge isn't one belonging to a sword and the frontier isn't to the end of the earth," Eve grumbled.

The faculty grew to six as Louis Alexander Dugas, Paul Fitzgerald Eve and John Dent joined. Twenty-seven students signed up for academic year 1832-33 in response to upgrading the faculty and curriculum. Doctor Dent stayed only one year. To fill his vacancy, Antony's son-in-law Ignatius Garvin returned from hiatus. This group of physicians became the nucleus of the school for years to come.

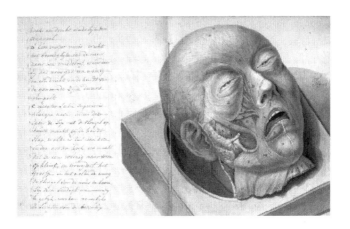

Chapter 4

Plagiarism & Publication

1835

Adam C's thesis on the subject of bleeding began, "When hemorrhage takes place from a large artery in one of the limbs, where the vessel can be conveniently compressed about the wound, a tourniquet, judiciously applied, never fails in putting an immediate stop to the bleeding. Before the invention of this instrument, which did not take place until the latter part of the seventeenth century, surgery was really a defective art. No important operation could be undertaken on the extremities, without placing the patient in the most imminent peril and the want of the aid, afforded by the tourniquet made many wounds mortal, which otherwise would not have been attended with the least danger."

The first weeks in April were dedicated to reading student theses and oral examinations in preparation for graduation. George B and Daniel D were tested and approved. Adam C's thesis rested on Doctor Dugas' desk. Something about his submission troubled the faculty. Although the subject met the broad stipulation of a work on the science of medicine, there was quiet questioning about the authenticity of composition by the student. The wording gave way to something familiar, yet not easily distinguished. Dugas went on a search, like a hunter on safari. The school library's founder searched through the jungle of anatomy, the rain forest of physiology and the plains of medical surgical practice until he found the rhino lying in the brush.

To the Friday, April tenth meeting, Doctor Dugas carried both Adam C's thesis and the *Dictionary of Practical Surgery* by Samuel Cooper. The two volumes were described as a complete exhibition of the present state of the principles and practice of surgery collected from the best and most original sources of information. A member of the Royal College of Surgeons in London, Doctor Cooper's work was published in New York in 1834.

"Gentlemen, I have discovered the source of our consternation. Adam C's thesis is an almost literal transcription from Samuel Cooper's work." Doctor Dugas had taken aim at close range, shot the beast and it lay motionless on display before the other professors. He read aloud to compare the writings and it was agreed to be exactly the same except for an occasional word change.

"Let it be resolved whereas Adam C has presented as an original thesis a production not of his own hand, he is thereby evidently guilty of plagiarism. He should not be considered an eligible candidate for the Doctorate." Unanimous agreement by the jury followed. It was decreed and a copy of the resolution was ordered to be sent to Adam C via the janitor, Mr. Clegg, who was himself under scrutiny for several accounts of intemperance and consequent incapacity. He'd been found in such a drunken stupor on two previous occasions that he was unable to clean the anatomy room. The professors continued on with their meeting. Alexander S and John T were examined and approved.

Mr. Clegg delivered the verdict of the misdeed and as Adam C read it, anger with accompanying flushing rose up from his toes to his chin. "The faculty has deemed." He fumed as he recalled sitting through their tiresome lectures, and studying endlessly to memorize their asinine requirements. How dare they tell him he is ineligible, he'd only borrowed some stupid words. Not all the words, just most, but he had at least learned while he copied. Was that not of import? His thoughts turned to his parents' efforts, their time and financial investment in his future career. What would they say? It would shame the family and they'd be furious. He'd lose face. His peers would loose respect for him. Adam C hoped he could convince the educators to overlook his freethinking. Begging, pleading, he would offer to create another thesis, this time with originality. He had certainly underestimated the wit and resourcefulness of the faculty. Accompanying the janitor back to the chambers, Adam C requested Mr. Clegg to implore the professors to hear his defense.

Forced to wait outside in the hall, he paced until they had completed their other business. Finally, Mr. Clegg ushered him into the roomful of men waiting to hear arguments to his case.

Doctor Dugas spoke, "Mr. C, our entire faculty, here, realizes that you presented a thesis which was not an original piece of work."

Adam C began his first sentence with a calm demeanor, "I understand that you gentlemen feel that I stole the words in my thesis." The young man stopped and looked from left to right at each of the seven professors seated behind the long, sturdy, oak conference table. They seemed unified in accusatory posture, most with arms crossed in front of their chests, as they stared back at him. He felt their judgment as though he reeked of some foul stench. Incensed once again at their attitudes, the hair on the back of his neck began to heat up and he felt as though they might burst into flame. Instead of his planned conciliatory remarks, Adam said, "And I would in turn charge you with injustice and ungentlemanly conduct in not having informed me of this matter sooner." He turned on his heels and abruptly left the room.

Doctor Antony shook his head, "How is it we could have informed him sooner? What a shame."

Monday came with an apology from Adam C. He expressed regret for his use of offensive language when he addressed the faculty and requested that he might be allowed to appear before them for an examination prior to the upcoming commencement, promising that he would present an original thesis that he hoped would prove satisfactory. His appeal was denied.

Fifteen graduates received their diplomas in the spring of 1835, but Adam C was not one of them. He had been the first student denied a diploma for such a heinous offense.

• • •

Doctor Antony's quest for increasing esteem for the medical profession was further evidenced in his brainchild publication of the *Southern Medical and Surgical Journal*, which began in 1836. Antony conceived of it to be a journal of practical information for Southern physicians; for those who practiced the healing arts in the country as well as the city. Its format was designed to consist of original articles and reviews as well as extracts from other journals. The first issue had contributions from Garvin, Dugas, Ford, and Antony. It was an opportunity for them to share their methodologies, such as Antony's treatment of leg fractures using counterweights. Previous methods of treatment left many a man lame. Milton Antony was a skilled practitioner and teacher eager to share his innovations.

Mr. D, a forty-six-year-old workman, was driving his wagon to town when his horse stumbled slightly. Thrown from his seat, he landed beneath the wagon in time for the left rear wheel to pass over his left thigh. The horse suffered no injury, but Mr. D felt searing pain and his lower leg appeared bent in a direction he wouldn't have thought possible. He had, with good fortune, fallen in proximity to the City Hospital. Doctor Antony was called to the street and brought two medical students with him to examine the downed man.

"This is a dislocation of the knee and a simple fracture of the femur of the left side, at the upper end of its lower third. We must reduce the dislocation and adjust the leg in place with temporary bandage and splints in order to move him into a bed in the hospital."

Antony sent the two students back to the hospital to gather supplies. He stayed with Mr. D and comforted the man. "We'll fix your leg for you, but you'll need to stay with us here in the hospital until it is healed. Is there someone you'd like us to notify about your accident?"

"Yes, please, sir. I work on the Bedford plantation, 'bout three miles west of here."

"Don't you worry, we'll send our janitor to take your horse and wagon back and tell your folks what's happened."

When the students returned, Doctor Antony demonstrated the manipulation of Mr. D's leg. After stabilization was achieved, Mr. D was placed on a litter and carried to his room.

The students placed him on his back in the bed, which had been outfitted with planks for firmness and then covered with blankets.

Antony sorted through some other supplies the students had brought in. "Here, now we must wrap these wooden slats into a six inch diameter cylinder with several coverings of cloth and place it under the upper third of his lower leg bone, the tibia. This must be far enough from the thigh as barely to touch it, and without pressure."

"Why are we doing that?" one of the students asked.

"The leg needs to be slightly elevated so that when we attach a weight it will pull freely on it."

A bandage was passed around the ankle in circular fashion several times and elongated into a figure eight to encompass the bottom of the foot where a string was attached. The string passed over the foot of the bed and extended six inches beyond the heel, so that a piece of brick weighing approximately two and a half pounds could be suspended.

"Now that we have the leg positioned, we must secure it."

Antony found four short splints and placed them on and at the sides of Mr. D's thigh.

"Now what is this called?" Antony held up a white colored binder with six extensions coming from each side.

"A many tailed binder?"

Antony cleared his throat. "That's one name for it, but what is the official, medical name?"

The two medical students looked at each other and winced.

"A scultetus binder," Antony clucked his tongue as if they should have known the answer to his question. He continued with his instructions, "We must put this on as snugly as possible without having it be constrictive. Here, lift the leg gently so that I may insert this squarely underneath, but do not change the angle of the leg."

The students strained to hold the leg firmly and up off the bed slightly, as their professor threaded the binder beneath.

Mr. D's thigh had become quite swollen and was beginning to show signs of bruising.

"What is the official term for swelling?"

"Tumefaction," one of the students answered quickly.

"And how do we treat it?"

"It needs to be kept moist with a solution of vinegar and water."

"Ah, finally, correct answers to my queries. I say this case will need further monitoring, but mainly for tightening of the scultetus binder as the tumefaction of his thigh decreases. In three weeks we will probably be able to remove the short splints and in five weeks his leg will be completely mended and we will be able to discharge him. We call this 'treatment of fracture by weight and fulcrum'."

Six months after Mr. D's accident, he stopped in at city hospital to express his gratitude. At Doctor Antony's request he performed maneuvers to demonstrate his agility by running in place and jumping. He was back at his work and had driven his wagon into town. Mr. D showed no sign of physical handicap and his recovery was impressive to medical students and colleagues.

Mr. D's case study plus other successful examples of Antony's traction techniques appeared in the first edition of the *Southern Medical and Surgical Journal*.

Chapter 5

Orientation

1838

Milton Antony always began orientation for incoming first year students by outlining the history of medicine and medical education in the state of Georgia. They reported to the intersection of Houston and Greene Streets in front of City Hospital. All thirty-nine new students were treated to a warm, sunny, blue-skied November morning in Augusta, as they huddled close to hear Antony's words.

"Good morning, and welcome to your first session at the Medical College of Georgia. Our commencements officially began on April seventeenth, eighteen-thirty-three, for our first four graduates of the complete two-year program. We hope that you will become one of our alumni as well. Behind me here is City Hospital." He turned and pointed to the two-story frame building with its pitched roof and chimneys extending at both ends. It was constructed in 1818 to serve the indigent sick. Originating as a ten-bed facility that could expand to twenty-one beds during epidemics, Antony began his teaching career in two apprentice rooms.

"I first became interested in medical licensure in eighteen-twenty-two. Several other colleagues joined me in founding the Medical Society of Augusta and it was this group who spoke up for the benefits of professional licensing. We went to the capital in Milledgeville and requested an appointment of a State Board of Medical Examiners. When it was enacted in eighteen-twenty-five, it provided that no person should practice medicine and surgery in Georgia without a license. I was actually chosen as the first chairman of the State Board. Can any one tell me the value of licensing physicians?"

A raised hand in the back of the group belonged to a young man named Robert Johnson. Antony pointed his finger in Robert's direction. "Yes, you there."

"Licensure is a means of regulating and setting standards. Otherwise what would prevent anyone from hanging up a sign and declaring themselves a physician?"

"You make an excellent point, sir. That is exactly what we wanted to accomplish. There is actually a specific group that concerns many of the licensed physicians in this state. Has anyone heard of Samuel Thomson?"

Antony looked at the group for a sign of recognition. Finding none, he continued. "Mr. Thomson has founded the Botanic School of Medicine. He sells his book along with the rights to use his remedies, composed of vegetable compounds, for the sum of twenty dollars. They are a roving band of quacks and certainly in direct opposition to Heroic medicine practiced and purported by Benjamin Rush at the turn of the century. Heroics is the brand of medicine taught in every respectable medical school, including ours." Antony's voice had taken on a judgmental and excited tone. It happened whenever he spoke of quackery.

"I began teaching in this very building in eighteen-twenty-six." He pointed again to City Hospital. "In the interest of maintaining high ideals, it seemed prudent to organize an institution for the purpose of regulating medical education as well. The powers of government were once again petitioned and permission was granted for the establishment of the Medical Academy. Governor Forsyth signed the enactment in December of eighteen-twenty-eight."

Robert raised his hand again.

"Do you have a question?"

"Yes, sir. How was medicine taught prior to the development of our Academy?"

"Generally medical education was personal, informal and consisted of an apprenticeship with a local physician. The preceptor shared his knowledge, treatments, and reference books, and the student's experience was gained by working in conjunction with him, reading and assisting in compounding his medicines. There was no set course of experience or specified time duration. Even if the local physician, turned instructor, had extensive training in the best schools under the finest teachers, instruction tended to remain local with experience and attitude centered on the immediate community. More ambitious wealthier students of medicine went to the north or overseas to attend their lectures. Does that satisfy your curiosity, young man?"

"Yes, sir."

"Class, we will not tour the interior of the hospital today, because there are so many of us and because you will see plenty of the inside of this building as your studies progress. We will walk the four blocks over to the Medical College building. Our plan is to talk more about history and the state of education. You will take a tour of our modern teaching facilities and be addressed by another of our original faculty members later today. Tomorrow will be the official introductory address to be delivered by our new Dean, Doctor Paul F. Eve. If there are no other questions, let's move on, and stay together now, so no one gets lost. "

Robert Johnson turned to one of his classmates, David Peters, and said, "I certainly hope no one gets lost within a four block radius."

David laughed softly, "Right. It might be a serious blot on our level of intelligence."

The two young men felt an instant bond and began sharing information as they walked.

"Where are you from?" Robert asked.

"Macon, and you?"

"Marthasville. Why, we're practically neighbors."

"Maybe we could attempt to study together." David was pleased to have found a friend.

"That idea appeals to me."

They arrived at the corner property at Telfair and Washington Streets, next to Richmond Academy with its one hundred and forty-foot frontage extending back to Walker Street. Dr. Antony motioned for the students to gather around him again as he perched on the top of the eight steps leading up to the mighty portico with front triangulated overhang and braced by six magnificent, ridged pillars. The building, in its Greek Revivalist splendor, had a domed temple-form structure.

"Here we are at the Medical College of Georgia. Our name was changed in eighteen-thirty-four, the same year the plans for the new building were drawn. Although City Hospital has and will continue to provide opportunities for bedside instruction, it was deemed to have inadequate teaching facilities. The General Assembly appropriated ten thousand dollars for the school to obtain a proper lot and begin constructing a building suitable for medical education. This is the result of that effort. It was not without difficulties, however. The building took longer to materialize than was originally proposed. Charles Cluskey was the architect and although we had construction problems and delays, we're quite pleased and proud of our edifice, which has been declared an ornament to both the city and the state. Enter through this double door." Antony opened the tall passageway and made a welcoming gesture to his future medical successors.

They stepped into the interior featuring a large rotunda with a solid circular mahogany staircase leading to the second story where lecture rooms, laboratory, library and museum were all designed to be heated by an innovative system of hot air pipes.

David nudged Robert and pointed to several water streaks on the sides of the walls leading to two buckets on the floor. "It looks as though there's been some leaking in the mighty building."

Doctor Antony saw the gesture, and although he hadn't heard the comment, he explained. "One of our peskiest problems has been the persistence of a leaky roof. It actually led to a reduction in the negotiated final bill and it obviously still continues to leak occasionally. Follow me." Antony made a sweeping motion in the air, led the way up the stairs and ushered the students into a classroom with straight backed chairs, exactly the number needed for each class member. "I'm now going to turn this class over to Doctor Garvin, who will continue your overview."

Ignatius Poultney Garvin was a man of six-foot height with hazel eyes. He had a moderately sized nose and mouth and his long face stopped abruptly with a squared-off projecting chin. His fair complexion suited his sandy-colored hair. A graduate of the Medical College of South Carolina, he settled in Augusta and married Doctor Antony's daughter in 1826.

"Good morning everyone. I trust Doctor Antony has warmly welcomed you all, as do I. I will begin by explaining the conditions necessary for graduation. You must have attended two courses in this institution, or one course in another respectable medical college or university and one in this institution. Candidates for the degree of Doctor of Medicine must attain the age of twenty-one, produce satisfactory testimonials of good moral character and deliver an originally written thesis on a medical subject to the dean of the faculty two weeks before the annual meeting of the board of trustees. We will let you know exactly when that will be in plenty of time for you to prepare. Fees are required to be paid in full; course fees are to be paid directly to each professor and you students, in return will receive tickets, which allow entry. As an example, you would pay fifteen dollars to Doctor Dugas to attend his surgery course. A full set of tickets will cost one-hundred-twenty dollars and will cover all the courses including anatomy, chemistry, surgery, institutes and practices, material medica and midwifery. Additionally, there is a matriculation fee of three dollars and a fee of ten dollars assessed for the demonstration of anatomy. After obtaining a set of tickets, your names will be entered in the registry book. Does anyone have any questions?"

David raised his hand. "Sir, what will be the total cost for the two years?"

"Well, let's calculate the mathematics. That is one-hundred-thirty-three dollars for the first year and there is an additional thirty dollar fee in the second year assessed for your diplomas," Garvin cleared his throat, "should you succeed..." He peered around the room to check their attention level. "So that will amount to, for the two years, a total of two-hundred-ninety-six dollars."

"Thank you, sir," David said. "I certainly hope to succeed."

"Yes, of course. That is what all the professors here want."

Money from the ticket sales was turned over from faculty members to the dean, who then divvied out the monetary compensation for teaching with the amount that was left over after meeting all other expenses.

Garvin continued, "And you will be attending school for a five-month term. Our previous Dean, Doctor Lewis DeSaussure Ford, had put forth an attempt to increase the term to six months. He had circulated letters to fifteen of what were considered the outstanding medical colleges in the United States, looking to the University of Pennsylvania as the preeminent institution. His suggestion was to call a national forum to discuss an official standard length. However, as an idea perhaps ahead of its time, it has not been well received. We have settled for five months."

There existed a lack of cooperation among medical schools, which resulted in varying lengths of courses and controversy over developing a standard. The Medical College of Georgia was endeavoring to adhere to six-month sessions, but most others required only four months worth of lectures.

Students clamoring for the shortest possible school terms made competition for candidates keen between Southern and Northern medical schools, an early foreshadowing of broader tensions.

"We will tour the library shortly, but let me first tell you of its history. Doctor Dugas, whom you all will become acquainted with as the 'father' of the library, acquired his much-deserved name by traveling to Paris with six thousand dollars. He returned from Europe in September, eighteen-thirty-four, with many of the latest medical volumes by prominent European physicians and surgeons, a variety of teaching aids and apparatus that will be used and are of enormous value to the faculty in their daily lectures."

Dugas collected a one-thousand-dollar contribution from each faculty member. The funds were raised without much apparent difficulty as he sailed six weeks after the trip was authorized. "One more thing, as we read and write case studies, there is a rule about using a patient's real name for reasons of confidentiality. We avoid that by substituting a letter of the alphabet for their surname. We say Mrs. S, for example."

The Medical College of Georgia was developing a reputation at a national level, not merely local or state. With its proud new building and increasing enrollment, the school's physicians found that they had to uncover a reliable supply of dissection material.

George M. Newton, a graduate of the University of Pennsylvania, joined the faculty when it was expanded to eight in 1837. His title, Professor of Physiology and Pathological Anatomy, made him the demonstrator of anatomy. Although dissection remained illegal, medical schools sought cadavers as the only way of teaching about the human body. Shortly after Newton's arrival, Mr. Clegg was trained as a resurrectionist. He earned the sum of seventy-five cents per body and was esteemed to be competent by Doctor Newton. It was imperative that his operations, conducted mostly in the Cedar Grove Cemetery, remain a secret.

Not a part of the orientation day tour, an additional building had been erected in the yard behind the new Medical College building in 1837. It was specifically for body dissections.

Chapter 6

Yellow Fever

1839

Seized with the sensation of a chill, Paul Gardner sat straight up in bed. As his bedroom remained shrouded in darkness, he surmised that it was sometime in the middle of the night. A dull pain spread from his forehead to behind his eyes and he noted stiffness in his thigh muscles. Gently fluffing his pillow, he turned over and covered his shoulders tightly up to his neck until he felt the blanket hem, all quietly done so as not to disturb his wife, Amanda, as she slept next to him. He hoped it wasn't happening to him. Fitfully, he dozed until the first light of day streamed in through a slit between the two heavy dark green velvet drapery panels at the window.

He'd been summoned two weeks earlier to attend to his patient, Mr. F, the fifth case of the strange fever malady. General medical practice of the day was based on a belief that the body contained four humors; blood, phlegm, yellow bile and black bile. Sickness and disease occurred when one or more of the four humors were out of balance. The imbalance was believed to be caused by miasmas; a noxious or unpleasant vapor that either traveled through the air, flowed through water or was present underground. The goal of the physician was to bring the humors back into balance. Physicians assisted their patients by expelling the ill humor through bleeding, or giving laxatives, emetics, diuretics, diaphoretics, or plasters. These therapies were also used in combination.

Cathartics were powerful laxatives used to cleanse the bowels. Evacuation of the bowels was also accomplished with enemas. Emetics were used to cause vomiting to cleanse the stomach. For promotion of the discharge of urine, diuretics were used.

Diaphoretics created free and copious perspiration.

Bloodletting was accomplished either by venesection, whereby a vein was cut open to allow bleeding to occur, or by a localized method using small superficial cuts for blood to be removed. At times, using the former method, patients would be bled until they fainted.

Another common thought of the day was that discomfort produced in one area of the body reduced pain in another. Application of a plaster made of a powder such as mustard and mixed with liquid for spreadability was intended to cause great irritation to the skin.

When Doctor Gardner arrived on that first morning, he noted Mr. F's pulse to be strong and full at one hundred twelve beats per minute and his temperature elevated at one hundred three degrees.

A man of thirty-five, Mr. F complained, "I have a headache cutting across my forehead and no appetite."

"How long have you had the ague… the fever?"

"It must be two days now and my muscles pain me

all over, but my back is the worst with an ache running down into my legs, here." Mr. F pointed to his thighs.

On physical examination Doctor Gardner further noted Mr. F's tongue had a milky white coating with an ominous yellowish color change toward the back of his mouth. Red edges and a red diamond were apparent on the tip. His eyes showed bloodshot streaks, upper lip puffed out and cheekbones displayed a faintly purplish tint. Mr. F had a quintessential case of Yellow Fever.

Three compound cathartic pills were given at once to the patient with several sips of water. Two small packages containing mustard and salt were given to Mrs. F as she was directed to give a hot footbath with the ingredients, while the physician retrieved his bloodletting instrument case with the brass scarificator, glass cups and brass syringe.

While his feet soaked, Doctor Gardner rolled up Mr. F's right nightshirt sleeve. The patient's forearm skin was sponged with warm water to increase blood flow to the area. The physician took the spring-loaded scarificator; an instrument shaped like a three-inch square box, and placed it on the arm. Mr. F looked away. When Doctor Gardner pressed down on the spring release, several small blades previously concealed were unleashed. The spring lancets perforated the skin and cut just below the skin surface into blood vessels. The cupping glass was then placed over the cuts and suction applied with the syringe. After five ounces of blood was extracted, the cup was removed and the wound dressed with lint and plaster.

Doctor Gardner upheld his physician's duty to be observant, cheerful, hopeful, positive and frank, but not necessarily truthful. He was careful not to mention the dreaded diagnosis to Mr. F, and he kept back the actual degree of his temperature. He knew he must convince his patient that he was not very sick; certainly not suffering with the prevailing fever.

The doctor next gave a coal-tar derivative with some bicarbonate of soda to keep his fever down and prevent nausea, followed by an enema to prevent constipation. He passed a well-oiled rectal tube as far up the bowel as possible and with a fountain syringe slowly forced two pints of warm soapy water to cause evacuation with Mr. F seated on a commode.

Further instructions were given to Mr. F's wife. She was to repeat the oral coal-tar remedy every three to six hours, wipe her husband's hands and face frequently, and give him hot lemonade to drink as he could tolerate. If he complained of being hungry, she was advised to put a pot of rice water on the stove and keep it boiling as he could eat that freely in both quantity and frequency as desired.

Doctor Gardner indicated that he would return at the same time tomorrow.

As he left the F's house on Lincoln Street near the Savannah River, he noticed the putrid smell of rotting garbage hanging thickly in the air. The riverbed had been extraordinarily low due to drought conditions and the enormous garbage dump near the northern part of the city was more odorous than usual. Paul Gardner conjectured that the fever might somehow be coming from there. He'd heard other proposed causes such as rotting tropical fruit, atmospheric conditions, or that the disease targeted those prone to filth. Still other theorists blamed the spread from those already infected. It was an unknown.

On Doctor Gardner's second visit to Mr. F, the man looked remarkably recovered. He was sitting up in bed and claimed to feel "fit as a fiddle," but the physician spoke with words of caution.

"I want you to stay calm and quiet for the next three

days. Only then will we rejoice at your full recovery. I am encouraged, but you must continue to take your medication and I will come by to see you again the day after tomorrow."

As Mr. F seemed more comfortable, Doctor Gardner took his wife out into the hall and spoke with her.

"There is a tendency for venereal desire during early convalescence. I must most strongly urge against it. I am warning you that even though he may seem to be improving greatly, I have heard and seen that too early a conjugal encounter could lead to his demise."

Mrs. F nodded her understanding. "He will be kept quiet and unexcited."

On Doctor Gardner's third visit to Mr. F, the horror of imminent collapse was evident. The black vomit had begun and whether the cause was from stomach excess, faulty food, the skin chilling or hearing unwelcome news, whatever the origin of the collapse, the outcome was the same.

Doctor Gardner never attended a patient's funeral.

On August 19, 1839, following a consultation between the mayor and physicians of Augusta, an official announcement was made. An epidemic of Yellow Fever had seized the city.

It was that same day Paul Gardner woke up with his symptoms. His pain now extended to behind his knees and into the calves of his legs. He tried to sit up on the edge of the bed, but every nerve ending seemed raw and he fell back down on the mattress, his body not willing to move. Restless and uncomfortable, he dreaded the conversation. His wife was already dressing for the day. "Amanda, I am not well. I woke in the middle of the night with a chill and now I fear the fever…the dreaded fever."

"Shall I send for Doctor Antony?"

"Please do."

Word returned from the Medical College that Milton Antony would be unable to respond to Doctor Gardner as he was afflicted by the fever himself. He had worked tirelessly with the ailing and mistakenly thought that with the fever, death was only associated when it was in conjunction with another medical condition.

Augusta's population estimate was six thousand five hundred and nearly one-third were reported to have Yellow Fever. Of those two thousand cases, deaths numbered two hundred forty.

Milton Antony and Paul Gardner both succumbed. Doctor Antony was fifty years old at the time of his death. His grave and marker were placed on the grounds of the campus of the college to make provision for its proper care by those left behind, his younger associates. His death caused a suspension in the publication of the *Southern Medical and Surgical Journal*. He had been the leading force for the Medical College and his passing left a gaping hole in its administrative and academic members, like a ship at sea battle hit by a giant cannon ball. The remaining faculty rallied to keep the ship from sinking. Amanda Gardner stayed in "heavy" mourning for two full years. To the edge of her outermost petticoat she added a dark band to prevent any white from showing through underneath the hem of her black dress.

Fall classes at the Medical College began two weeks late. The physicians who had cared for the sick and survived, suffered from exhaustion. Because of the unknown causative agent for yellow fever, suitable subjects for anatomy classes had to be imported. One hundred dollars worth of cadavers were ordered from New York. The bodies were shipped in brine by boat to Charleston and then transported by railroad to Hamburg, South Carolina, the city across the Savannah River from Augusta.

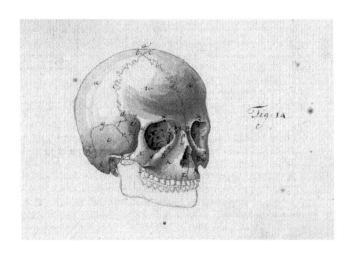

Chapter 7

An Evil Spirit

1854

In the two years Grandison Harris had been performing his job of obtaining specimens for the Medical College, he'd never had a problem with Bessie bolting away before. He couldn't get the horse to slow down until they were almost back to the Cedar Grove Cemetery entrance. It seemed as if the old mare had a mind of her own and she wouldn't stop sprinting until she'd gotten to a place where she knew she could rest again.

John had gotten so jostled in the wagon's burst of speed he wasn't able to find his way out of the burlap bag, but as the buckboard slowed he began to wriggle free. When Bessie stopped completely at the gravesite, Grandison saw the movement in the bag.

He stood up, picked up his shovel and said, "Dis be evil spirits at work . . . you's supposed to be dead. I's making

sure of it," and with a heavy hand swung the shovel
down on the writhing bag.

A shriek escaped from the sack, and then silence.

"That'll be the end of you and now back into that box
you goes. I was gonna' take you over to Doc Campbell's
lab. You's supposed to be getting cut up in the morning.
I's supposed to get you on one of his tables. I's only come
back here to cover up this hole. I don't sees how you
could've gotten you's soul back, but all I knows is you is
too spirited for me to take to de school and I sure don't
wants you in my wagon 'cause I ain't for sure you is
dead yet. I's putting you back into the ground where you
comes from."

Harris stepped into the back of the wagon and grabbed
the sack with its limp contents. "Something sure seems
different...you feels lighter than you was before. Must be
that evil spirits all gots knocked out of you. No, I ain't
takin' no chances. That spirit still gots to be around here
somewhere. If he gits back in you'll rise up again. Old doc
will have to come and get you himself if he really wants
you. I's done with dis whole business, I's too scared."

He skillfully pushed the bag and contents back into
the earthen tunnel from which he had pulled his haul
earlier. Although in a hurry, he knew he needed to make
everything look as undisturbed as possible. He smoothed
over the dirt, replaced the yellow marigolds and covered
his footprints, in spite of his shaken state.

Grandison returned to the buckboard, pulled a flask
from his coat and took another swig of whiskey. "Bessie,
what gots into you tonight? Was you scared by that spirit,
too? I knows that the doc says there ain't none. He being
a God fearing, Bible reading man and I does want to
believe him, but sometimes I don't knows. Especially, like
tonight when it looked like we has a real evil one with us
right here in this wagon. All of that moanin' and wigglin'

in that sack. I still gots the shivers." He coaxed the horse to begin her trek back to their lodgings.

It was nearly a mile from Cedar Grove Cemetery on Watkins Street to the Medical College located on the corner of Telfair and Washington Streets. Grandison let the horse find her own pace. She clomped slowly through the dusty streets while he regained his senses.

After the porter positioned the wagon by the anatomy lab door near the keeping room, he fed and stabled Bessie. Adjacent to the stable, his sparsely decorated quarters with cot, small storage chest, wash basin, and chamber pot awaited. Before retiring for the night, he drank a few more comforting belts of whiskey to calm his nerves.

Chapter 8

Canal Design

1845

Cotton farming had sustained the Adams family for years. Sterling's grandfather, Sebastian Adams began with a small plot of land in 1790. He had not only witnessed the demonstration of the first cotton gin, he had participated in the green seed mania.

"Gentlemen, apply to my young friend, Mr. Whitney. He can make anything." The year was 1793 and the speaker was Catherine, the widow of the Revolutionary War hero, Nathaniel Greene. She referred to Eli Whitney, possessor of an extraordinary understanding of mechanics. At her encouragement, he studied the cotton cleaning process. Displaying wide shoulders, big hands and a gentle manner, Whitney had worked as a blacksmith, nail maker and supplier of ladies' hat pins prior to attending Yale University. After graduating at the age of twenty-seven with a teacher's degree, he was hired by Catherine Greene to tutor her children at Mulberry Grove plantation, near Savannah, Georgia.

"I will develop a machine to separate green seed cotton lint from its small tough germs." Whitney studied the hand movements and simulated them with his machine.

When he showed off his prototype, he explained, "To do the lint pulling work of the fingers, I have a drum rotate past the sieve, see here, almost touching it." Eli pointed to the drum. "On the surface of this drum, fine hook-shaped wires project which catch and pull the lint away from the seed. The restraining wires of the sieve hold the seeds back while the lint is pulled away. A rotating brush then cleans the lint off the hooks. And look, we have cranked out the equivalent of a full day's work for several pair of hands in just one hour!"

With the promise of this new technology, which Whitney dubbed the 'cotton gin,' planters ordered their fields to be sowed with green seed cotton, including Sebastian Adams. "What a fantastic feat of engineering," was his proclamation. "I will plant all my fields with green seed cotton." As word spread, planters agreed exponentially.

Phineas Miller, Whitney's partner, first proposed installing the machines and charging farmers a fee for doing their ginning, amounting to two-fifths of the profit to be paid in cotton. The farmers resented the idea.

Sebastian Adams spoke to several of his planter friends, "If we have an abundant cotton crop that comes to harvest, rather than drown in a sea of white fiber, I suggest we find another option. I'm opposed to outright piracy just as much as I'm opposed to robbery. The fees proposed for using their machines are excessive…it is downright thievery. But we all saw how Eli Whitey's gin worked. It was a simple design. We could create the same type of model. He has no patent yet. And I've heard he is embroiled in all sorts of legal wrangling."

Compelled by a bumper crop of the billowy white plants sitting on his fields waiting to be harvested, Sebastian Adams and others copied Whitney's gin design.

Litigious disputes followed. Whitney obtained his patent in 1794 and Miller proposed taking payments by levying a one pound cotton tax for every three pounds produced. Again, the planters were outraged, including Sebastian Adams. Imitations of Whitney's machine continued to appear and because of a loophole in the patent act wording, costly suits against pirates and the owners of the imitations went unsettled.

"They'll never get us," were the words of Sterling's grandfather.

Whitney and Miller then sought to settle for outright sale or modest royalty on machines made by someone else. During the struggle, in 1796, Miller married Mrs. Greene and subsequently moved to Cumberland Island, Georgia. The Carolinas, Tennessee and Georgia levied taxes on the cotton gins in their states and collections amassed nearly ninety thousand dollars. By that time, however, Whitney and Miller owed most of that money in legal fees or other expenses. Another financial blow came in 1803, when the states rescinded their agreements and sued the partners for all the monies that had been paid to them. Miller died in that year.

In 1804 Whitney applied to federal Congress for relief and was saved from total ruin. He was thirty-nine years old, penniless, and exhausted. Whitney turned his back on cotton, the cotton gin and the South. That same year the cotton crop earned planters nearly ten million dollars. Sebastian Adams was one of the profiteers. He bought more and more land with his earnings. When he died in 1842, he owned some four hundred acres which he willed to his only son, Sterling's father, George Adams.

• • •

Drought challenged the stability of the South. It was not only a drought on agricultural stability caused by a lack of rain, but a drought on social stability caused by a lack of progressive thinking. Industrialization was occurring at a dizzying pace in the North. Cotton was grown in the South and sent to a port city for transport to the North. It was made into cloth in northern mill factories and then shipped back down South at double the price. It made little sense to creative thinkers like Henry Hartford Cumming who resided in Augusta, Georgia in 1845. "I realize that while cotton can't be grown in the North because of climate restrictions, factories could and certainly should be built in the South."

Opponents of Cumming argued, "The loss of the agricultural Southern lifestyle directed by the seasons will be replaced with tolling bells to divide up the mill workers' day and we will become exactly like our loathsome neighbors in the industrialized North. Overcrowding will occur like in Northern factory towns. Industrialization will reduce the culture of the South."

Men with thoughts of southern nationalism and independence were called upon for support.

But, Henry Cumming turned his sights up river from Augusta, where a transition in geography takes place. Rocky shoals of the Savannah River mark the area where the piedmont plateau meets the Atlantic coastal plain. The river flows three hundred miles through forests, agricultural lands and swamps before it empties into the Atlantic Ocean near Savannah. In order to power industry, water has to drop; falling water contains the energy to drive machines. The city of Augusta lay on the fall line where the river dropped fifty two feet in elevation over six miles as it left the hard rock of the piedmont and hit the soft rock of the coastal plain. It seemed perfect.

Cumming was an introspective and retiring man who, after obtaining a liberal education and traveling in Europe for three years, began the practice of law with George Crawford. Henry Cumming was not only living in the golden age of canals, he was convinced that the Savannah River offered opportunities for waterpower.

"We do not need a canal in Augusta for transportation, as steamboats carry most of our trade on the Savannah River. We need a canal for water power."

Following construction of the Erie Canal in 1825, the United States had a case of canal fever, but Augusta's neighboring state of South Carolina was investing in railroads. Economic times were difficult. There had been a national depression in 1837 and businesses declined. Recovery was slow. The abilities of the South were challenged.

Cumming rebounded, "I will rely on the argument of Southern Pride with the idea of turning the regions' own cotton into cloth to compete with industrial might of the North. A comparative analysis shows that the South has a more favorable climate with the proper humidity for manufacturing textile fibers, open waterways year-round with no ice, cheap water power and plenty of willing laborers."

Lowell, Massachusetts, became a model city for the creative thinkers in Augusta, Georgia. "The Lowell of the South" became the mantra for Cumming and other potential growth seekers.

"Why not spin as well as plant cotton? The same hand that attends the gin may work a carding machine. The girl who is capable of making thread on a country spinning wheel may do the same with equal facility on the throstle frame. The woman who can warp the thread and weave it on a common loom may soon be taught to do the same on a power loom and so with all departments from the raw cotton to the cloth, experience has proven that any child, white or black, of ordinary capacity may be taught in a few weeks to be expert in any part of a cotton factory. It is only necessary to build a manufacturing village of shanties, in a healthy location, to have crowds of these poor people around you seeking employment at half the compensation given to operatives in the North." William Gregg wrote his famous essay in January, 1845.

In that same year, the census of the city of Augusta counted three thousand nine hundred forty-eight whites, four hundred forty free colored, three thousand one hundred-fourteen slaves, two deaf, one dumb and seven lunatics. This same city charged the Canal Board of Commissioners to construct a watercourse. Funding came from four banks advancing seed money, and the City Council of Augusta issued bonds. Residents were forced to pay a special canal tax to retire the debt. Some taxpayers filed suit, but lost.

Henry Cumming hired J. Edgar Thomson, a prominent railroad engineer. He charged him to "Complete a survey for a canal. Write up your appraisals and divide the work."

Thomson returned with his assessment, "I have done exactly as you asked. The canal work has been divided into twelve sections at three different levels. I also recommend that you employ a local engineer, William Phillips, and dedicate him to the operation of the canal and the water works."

On April, 25, 1845, Henry Cumming announced, "The contracts are all assigned, with the exception of section one; the headgates."

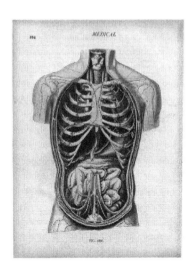

Chapter 9

Mesmerism vs. Anesthesia

Louis Alexander Dugas and Paul Fitzgerald Eve were both men of surgery. They had been hired by the Medical College of Georgia as such, both stately gentlemen and skilled lithotomists, they not only displayed speed in their craft; they often worked together, shared surgical techniques and were like-minded on many issues except one. Doctor Dugas became convinced of the power of mesmerism while Doctor Eve waited for news of the newer substances of ether and chloroform. They bantered on until their beliefs about reducing a patient's sensibilities during surgery became the subject of a friendly debate.

On the third of January 1845, Mrs. G presented herself to Doctor Dugas' office.

"Sir, I have been referred to you for examination of this growth," as she pointed to the right side of her chest.

"Madam, how long have you had this tumor?"

"It has been present and gradually increasing in size for three years. Doctor Cornwall most recently likened it to the size of a turkey's egg and I have been advised to have it removed. It is on his recommendation that I have come to this city for that purpose."

"I will thank him for his referral and I agree completely with his advice. Madam, does it cause you any discomfort?"

"No, sir."

Doctor Dugas examined the woman and found the three inch cone-shaped mass over her right breast.

"And would you say your health has been fairly robust and not impaired by this growth?"

"Yes, sir, that is the truth. I must confess, though I am quite frightened by the prospect of going under the knife. I am a cowardly sort."

"Not at all, the fear of intolerable pain challenges most people's resolve. What is your age and have you borne any children?"

"I am forty-seven and have had no children, sir."

"I think we should operate tomorrow."

"Doctor Dugas, I am staying here with a family friend, Mr. H, who has urged me to consider mesmerism. I must admit that I know nothing about it, but I am compelled to ask and would seek and certainly abide by your advice."

"Dear lady, I am aware of several authenticated cases where mesmeric influence has been successfully used to alter the consciousness of a patient undergoing surgery. Mesmerism, also called animal magnetism, would be quite interesting to observe and I could be enrolled in its use, should it prove effective. I would first need to make a test for suitability in your case, and I propose endeavoring to mesmerize you tomorrow rather than perform the surgery."

"Thank you so much sir, I am staying at Mr. H's house

on Greene Street."

"Yes, I am familiar with Mr. H's house. I will see you there at eleven o'clock tomorrow then."

Mr. H met Mrs. G when she returned from her appointment, "What did he say about mesmerism?"

"He will be coming by tomorrow morning to investigate my receptiveness."

"Let us see about your receptiveness right now. I'll perform it on you."

"All right, what do I have to do?"

"Sit in this chair and arrange yourself comfortably. There are several ways to accomplish this task, so long as we create a magnetic field."

He walked to his bookcase and retrieved a small wooden box. From it he removed a metal rod, one inch in diameter and five inches long.

"Now, sit back and look at me. I'm going to make a series of passes in front of you and I want you to watch the wand."

Mr. H slowly and methodically moved the rod in a full arm's length motion, sweeping like a pendulum in front of Mrs. G. It took Mr. H more than fifteen persistent, but patient minutes before Mrs. G's eyelids began to appear heavy. She began to snore and he left her quietly in her somnambulistic state for some time until he pronounced, "I will count backward from ten and as I do you will come from that very deep place where you are now. Ten, you are rising up from that deep place. Nine, think of walking up a flight of stairs. Eight more to go. Seven, you are becoming aware of the room you are in. Six, you can smell the fire burning. Five, you are feeling lighter and Four, even lighter. Three, you are almost to the top of the stairs. Two, when I snap my fingers, you will awaken fully and have no memory of having slept. One..."

Clicking his middle finger and thumb together, Mrs. G's

eyes opened exactly as he'd commanded.

"When shall we begin?"

"'Tis already done, dear lady."

When Doctor Dugas arrived the next morning, Mr. H related their success story.

"What do you believe of this, Mrs. G?"

"Doctor, I have no memory of the events of last night and as such I am hoping to prove that I will be a suitable candidate."

"Very well then." It was Doctor Dugas' turn to try and place Mrs. G into a hypnotic trance. He accomplished it in a different, yet no less successful way.

"Mrs. G, I want you to rest comfortably against the back of your chair and I will sit on this stool here. Now gently close your eyes and imagine that you are standing in a glade at the edge of a beautiful wooded path. You will journey into this peaceful and primitive place becoming more deeply entranced as you venture further along the path. Look around at the beautiful trees with their leaves surrounding you. There is a babbling brook to your right and farther up on your left is a serene pond with pink water lilies. It is so peacefully quiet and calm. You are becoming more and more relaxed."

The physician's soothing voice led Mrs. G into a deep, mesmeric trance. He allowed her to stay there as he spoke to Mr. H.

"I am quite impressed with her receptiveness to suggestion. However, I do not believe it prudent or convenient that I be the one and same individual to perform both the trance and the surgery. I will require your assistance, Mr. H. And beyond that, I would request that you continue to mesmerize Mrs. G in the morning and evening hours until insensibility is induced. I believe this will increase her ability to arrive at a hypnotic state with less and less delay. I will continue to monitor this process and will decide on a surgical date based on how this progresses."

"I will abide by your directions, sir," said Mr. H.

"Excellent. Let's wake her up."

Doctor Dugas went around to the back of Mrs. G's chair. He spoke with no inflection in his voice, "Dear lady, you are to come out of the woods now. Walk back on the path toward the glen where you entered. Walk past the water lily pond, the babbling brook, and the grove of trees. You are back on the path, coming out of the woods. You will have no recollection of your walk. Coming back into this room in your parlor, you are rejoining me in your state of consciousness." Doctor Dugas snapped his fingers.

"Mrs. G. How do you feel?"

"Quite well and thank you Doctor. Have I been put under the effect again? I have no memory."

"Yes and I would say with continued success. I have instructed Mr. H to persist with your inductions regularly and I would like you to come to the office again day after tomorrow."

When Mrs. G and Mr. H visited the office on the eleventh of January 1845, Doctor Dugas had requested professional consultations to verify his findings. Thus, Doctors Ford and Means were in attendance. Mr. H demonstrated his facility of inducing Mrs. G into her trance state. With their practice, they had become more adept as he was able to touch her lightly on the forehead and in less than a minute she would melt into a deep state of hypnosis. As this was accomplished, Doctor Dugas took out his pocketknife and made a two-inch long by half-inch deep incision in her leg. The other two physicians looked on, amazed, as she seemed to have no sensation of the gash. Completely convinced that Mrs. G could undergo her surgery in a mesmerized state, the surgeon bandaged her cut.

The next day Mrs. G was returned to Doctor Dugas, unaware of the planned activities. She was entranced and moved to the operating theatre. In attendance were Doctors Means, Ford, Garvin and Newton. Noticeably absent was Doctor Paul Fitzgerald Eve.

Mr. H spoke up as the surgeon began to prepare, "Excuse me, Doctor Dugas, but I have never witnessed a surgical operation before and I fear I might lose my self-possession. Would it be possible for me to be blindfolded?"

Doctor Means fashioned a blindfold from a handkerchief and positioned Mr. H to the left side of Mrs. G. "Why don't you maintain touch by holding her hand?"

Doctor Dugas addressed his colleagues, "Will you please note the frequency of her pulse and respiration, the color of her complexion and facial expressions all before, during and after this procedure in order to detect any change in her function or to see evidence of any pain?"

Two elliptical incisions were made, eight inches in length, dissecting and removing her entire right breast and its attached tumor.

Mrs. G showed no indication of sensation nor did any of the other physicians note even the slightest changes in any of her vital functions. She remained in the same sound sleep as before the knife was used. The surgeon applied a dressing to the wound and he removed the blindfold from Mr. H.

Mrs. G was awakened half an hour after the dressing had been applied. She engaged in cheerful conversation as if nothing had occurred.

"Madam, do you think I could have removed your breast while you were asleep without your knowledge?"

"Doctor, I really do not know what to think possible based on the various experiments that have been accomplished to date."

"I found you to be in the proper state to perform your operation today, Mrs. G."

She shook her head, until the surgeon took her hand and carried it to that part of her body to find it was no longer there.

"I can't believe it's been done without my knowledge or feeling. I had no idea it was to be done today. And now it has been completely removed." Mrs. G was on the verge of hysteria, with feelings hovering somewhere between violation and relief.

"We have witnesses who can attest to the fact that you made no moves and appeared to feel nothing. No drugs or pain relievers have been given. It is done."

Mrs. G wept as the other physicians offered their congratulations.

Doctor Dugas believed that mesmerism was a reality and hoped that the phenomena of mesmeric sleep would be studied and utilized for all those who might benefit from it.

Students became aware of the experiment through rumor and clamored to understand more about this important discovery. In order to educate them, a lively debate was staged between Doctors Eve and Dugas.

Eve: "What we are to discuss is the apparent state of trance produced by animal magnetism, known as Mesmerism and named after Franz Anton Mesmer, an Austrian physician. The practice was unanimously condemned by the commission appointed in eighteen-seventy-eight by the king of France to examine and report upon it. Never has it received any favor or approbation from any scientific or learned society whatever."

Dugas: "The Academy of Science in Berlin offered a prize worth upwards of six hundred dollars in eighteen-eleven for the best work on animal magnetism. In eighteen-fifteen, the Emperor of Russia appointed a committee of able physicians to investigate the subject and agreed that animal magnetism is an important agent. They recommended its practice to enlightened physicians and in the next year, a similar law passed in Denmark. The King of Prussia limited the practice solely to physicians in eighteen-seventeen."

Eve: "Mesmerism is not reality. It is a phenomenon ascribed as justly due to the imagination and excited feelings."

Dugas: "I have recently performed an operation on a patient, Mrs. G, who is the only person I have ever seen who not only expressed no pain, but honestly averred to having felt no sensation whatever during the operation."

Eve: "The non-expression of pain is no proof of its non-existence and there are conditions of the body and mind on which no suffering is evinced. They may feel no pain, independent of the state of mesmerism."

Dugas: "I hope as a medical philosopher not to offend anyone who does not share my own opinions. I wish not to violate propriety or courtesy, but merely ask nothing more than a fair hearing and an impartial judgment on this form of treatment."

Eve: "Mesmerism can neither be demonstrated nor abide the test of experience."

• • •

Paul Eve had passed the deanship on to George Madison Newton in 1844. Doctor Eve wanted to revive the *Southern Medical and Surgical Journal.* To ensure a steady flow of material, each faculty member was to submit either five pages of original matter or ten pages of translation for each issue or pay a fine of twenty dollars.

In the January 1845 issue, the first since Antony's

death, Doctors Eve and Dugas published their professional opinions about mesmerism. The two associates had found a point of contention, but in a small rural office in Jefferson, Georgia, experiments had already occurred that would put their debate to rest.

Chapter 10

Famine

Ireland, 1847

Potatoes had been the major food staple for the McLennan family as long as Molly could remember. She and her husband, Corey, had their little plot of land out behind the rented house planted with the starchy food. They leased the cottage from a British landholder as Catholicism prevented them from ownership. When Corey was alive, they even had fun growing potatoes. The babies came and their potato crop flourished.

Now a widow struggling to care for her three children Tommy, Maureen and the youngest baby Ana, Molly McLennan stared out of the front door of the cottage with its thatched roof. She did not know how she would continue to feed her family. Gazing out over the green rolling acres of Irish farmlands, the blighted vegetable crop was hidden from view. From what she'd heard, though, everyone's potatoes had the black rot. There'd been a lively discussion after Mass on Sunday. Kelly Mahoney said he'd heard that eating potatoes with the blight could make one sicker than going hungry. Paddy Callahan disagreed saying that a few rotten potatoes mixed with a little cow's blood and boiled with cabbage in a soup could keep up one's strength.

Molly felt her strength and her resolve slipping away. Any semblance of her former beauty was gone; her black hair had lost its sheen long ago. She looked down at her spindly fingers ground gray with dirt. Her skinny forearms nearly bared bone. Molly was tired, exhausted with the struggle, but she wanted to believe Paddy. She'd begged him for a cabbage and the cow's blood. More than enough of her own spoiled potatoes were dug from their small garden plot. She'd put the concoction to simmer in the kettle over the hearth hours ago.

Folks were dropping so fast the parish priests couldn't keep up with all the death. Proper burials were little more than fantasies and sometimes there were none at all. Molly would be asking for some prayers when Ana's time came, nothing more than prayers to send her baby daughter on her way.

Ana's eyes looked like black sockets as she lay still in the corner. Her stomach protruded out from under her shirt. She hadn't used the chamber pot or cried for more than a day now. When Molly tried to wake her last, there wasn't even a whimper, just a limp little body. Molly tried to make her comfortable. She'd wet her lips and rub her little hands. There was relief in her lack of response. Maybe Ana had gone beyond the suffering. Molly couldn't bring her back for more. She hoped it wouldn't be long now. Resigned to losing one she'd given life to, Molly couldn't bear to watch them all starve. Ana was only two years old, but she was a frail little thing. Corey had so loved his favorite, little daughter. Molly was glad he wouldn't be there to watch her passing.

Even if it was too late for Ana, Maureen and Tommy might make it if they could get away from the rotting potatoes, maybe to America. Weren't some benevolent folks sponsoring passage to the New World on the promise to work as maids or laundresses? She could get Tommy to work. He was almost eight years old now and he had a strong pair of hands. Maureen was only six, but she was a smart little girl. Some kind landlords were even donating passage for those who couldn't pay their rent. She wasn't sure how kind hers was; if he would send her to America or the workhouse.

Molly feared the workhouse more than starving. If the landlord came to evict her and the children, they'd have no choice. She'd heard it was nearly impossible to keep the family together if they were sent off to workhouses. She couldn't bear to think of losing all her children. One was enough. She'd heard of whole families who'd lost contact. Maybe it'd be a better fate to go on and starve.

Coming in from outside, Tommy looked at Molly's nod as he rested the shovel next to the front door. He wiped his forehead and then his hands with a dirty rag he had hanging out of the back of his pants. His shoes were beginning to fall apart, barely clinging to his feet.

"Here, Tommy, eat this," she spooned some of the liquid she'd prepared into a small bowl and set it in front of her son. His appetite matched his recent growth spurt.

Molly walked over to where Ana was curled in a fetal position. She bent down with her ear near the child's mouth and nose, listening for breath. When she heard none, her body began a rocking, writhing motion accompanied by soft sobs. She muffled her cries, waiting until Tommy had eaten. Molly picked up the flaccid body of her daughter and cradled her. She walked toward her boy who sensed his mother's need for comfort. They carried the baby together and walked out toward the fresh grave Tommy had dug earlier.

Maureen was walking sideways up the hill holding onto Father Callahan's hand.

When Molly saw the priest her sobs turned into wails. "Father, my baby's gone."

"She's gone to heaven to be with the good Lord, though, Miss Molly. She'll have no more suffering from hunger."

Maureen hugged her mother's straggly skirt hem. "Mama, are we all going to go to heaven, now?"

As Molly could find no words, she shook her head indicating a negative response to her daughter.

They walked together up to the little gravesite and Father Callahan pulled out his rosary and began his prayers.

Tommy placed the small body in his earthen dugout and began to cover the hole with dirt. He ritualistically passed the shovel to his mother and then his sister, and then to the priest; each one picking up and then tossing a scoop full of the rich black loamy soil into the grave.

Molly pulled a small cross out of her tattered dress pocket. She had fastened two sticks together with willow. She handed it to her son. "Place this up at the head of her grave. She was such a tiny young thing; she won't be needing a bigger marker."

The man of the cloth took Maureen's hand and squeezed it gently, "This is certainly a pestilence amongst our people."

"Father, what's a pestisis?"

"It's a big word now, isn't it darling? It means a destruction; a terrible thing."

"Mama, what are we going to do?" Maureen placed her hands on her hungry belly.

Molly composed herself, "Let's go back to the cottage. Father, I've made a pot of Paddy's soup recipe. Will you have a bit?"

"No thank you, Molly, you need to feed these children."

"Soup, Mama?" Maureen started to run toward the house.

"Maureen, wait for me. Mind that pot is hot. Tommy, go run after her before she burns herself up. I'm coming right behind you."

"Being hungry makes us all a bit loony, now don't it Molly? Better run on with them. I'll follow behind."

Molly started to run, but turned around and said, "Father, let me fix their soup bowls, then I'd like to talk with you."

Father Callahan took his pipe from his jacket pocket, tamped down the tobacco in it and lit a match. Standing near the front door with one foot up against the house, the other grounded, he held the flame over the bowl as he took several draws to get it started.

Molly came back outside. "There, now at least they'll have something on their stomachs." She was quiet as she deeply inhaled the scent of pipe smoke. "Oh, that tobacco pipe smells like fine cherries. It reminds me of Corey. Father, I must ask you now, or lose my nerve. Have you heard anyone in the parish speaking of arranging passage to America?"

"Well now, Mick Kelly was speaking of brokering just the other day. He's working with one of the shipping firms. I heard that passage is costing near ten dollars now and probably five dollars for the little ones."

"Do you know what he's requiring?"

"No, I don't, but I'd certainly encourage you to talk with him. I think he'll help you, if he can."

"Father, I seem to be at my wit's end. I'd rather die trying to do something different, than die doing the same stinking thing."

"Molly, you've just lost your youngest child. And I understand that you don't want to go through that again. I'll bet you could find Mick down at the pub."

"I may just do that after the little ones are asleep for the night. Thank you for your prayers for Ana."

"It's about all I can do these days, and it isn't nearly enough. I'll be taking my leave now. We must believe that God has some greater good in mind and he's helping us along the way, with the wind at our backs, even if we can't see it every minute."

Molly watched his pipe smoke trail back down the hill toward the village. The aroma lasted long after he disappeared from sight and reminded her of happier times.

Molly went back inside her shell of a house. Suddenly everything about it made her feel sick. They had to get away from it.

"Mama, did I hear you talking to Father Callahan about going to America?" Tommy quizzed her.

"Indeed you did, my Tommy boy. I want you and Maureen to go to sleep whilst I go down into town and talk with Mick Kelly. Father Callahan thinks he might be able to help us book passage. Wouldn't you like to go to the New World?"

"Anywhere, as long as we have something to eat," Maureen added.

"Alright then, be cooperative children and go to sleep. I'll tell you all about what I find out in the morning."

Molly remained in the house until her children fell asleep. While she waited, she ate a bowlful of Paddy's concoction. The first taste made her choke. She wondered how her children had endured something so awful, but her stomach's craving made her curious enough to try again. The second swallow went down easier.

By the time she'd finished the bowl, she heard snoring sounds. As she prepared to go to town, she noticed some increased strength, and she thought that maybe Paddy was on to something.

It was a half-mile walk into the village. For the first time in weeks, Molly felt a sense of hopefulness. She made it to McDougal's Pub and walked right inside. Once the door closed behind her, she realized that being a woman alone in a pub might not be the best thing. But, she knew most of the men drinking their rounds, as they all went to hear Father Callahan's homilies on Sundays. Molly set eyes on Mick Kelly sitting by himself over in a dark corner and she moved toward him. She had no money and hoped the bartender wouldn't require her to buy anything.

Molly thought Mick was a handsome man with his black curly hair and blue eyes. He was thirty-five and never married. Now his complexion had an ashen hue like everyone's.

She scooted between tables and made it over to where he was sitting.

"Hello, Love, what brings you here by me, tonight?"

"Hey, Mick. I've got a heavy weight upon my heart. My baby daughter, Ana, died today."

"Ah, this terrible famine, it's taking away all our loved ones. My Dad dropped over last week. Can I buy you a pint? There's strength in the ale."

"I'm so sorry to hear about your father. Yes, I'd like a drink."

"And I'm sorry to hear of your daughter." Mick raised his hand showing two fingers to the bartender.

"I was speaking with Father Callahan after he offered up his prayers for wee Ana and he said he'd heard that you were working for a shipper now and you might know something about booking passage to America."

The bartender set down two mugs of pale yellow ale.

"Really, well I wonder how he heard about that."

"You mean you're not?"

"Well, no I am, but I'm not advertising it. I thought about going myself, but my Mum is still living here and I can't travel right now. Did you want to go?"

"Mick, I'm desperate to go. I don't want to see Maureen and Tommy taking the same path as Ana."

"I understand."

There was an awkward moment of silence that Molly covered up with her drink. She took a big swig of the bubbly ale and swished it around in her mouth, savoring its freshness. She was beginning to feel warm all over.

"Do you know anything about making the voyage?" Mick asked.

Molly shook her head in an admission of ignorance. "Mick, it's just that staying here is a certain death sentence. Perhaps going to America is at least a different kind of sentence."

"I've been working as a broker with some of the merchants. That's what Father Callahan meant. They bring their ships over to dock in Galway. They unload their cargo and then put in berths for people. Instead of taking a half-empty ship back across the Atlantic, they're filling the holds up with émigré. It takes a month or more to get there though, Molly. And I don't want to paint you a rosy picture; the conditions aren't the best."

"Hey, Mick, have you seen the filth I'm living in now? And we have nothing to eat. How much does it cost?"

"Not everybody makes it either. Molly, you need to know that some ships lose almost half their passengers to sickness."

"I'll take my chances. How much does it cost? How can I find the money to get there?"

"Who's your landlord? Do you think he'd pay your

passage?"

"It's that stinky old Brit, Morgan. I don't want to ask him for nothing. I have a little pride left." Molly was beginning to sway as she sat in the booth.

"There is another way. I could sponsor you and you could pay me back once you find work. I've heard if you make it, it's easy to find work over there. I've made a little extra money lately, so I don't mind helping. There is a ship leaving Galway day after tomorrow and it's going to Savannah, Georgia."

"Oh, Mick, be a dear and get me and the kids on it. I promise we'll pay you back. Maybe I can even give you a little something now."

"I thought you didn't have any money."

"I don't, but that doesn't mean I can't give you a little something else."

Molly reached over and put her hand on Mick's thigh.

"Yeah, I guess that ought to be worth some kind of discounted ticket, but I don't expect you to prostitute yourself, Love."

"I'm just showing my gratitude is all."

He moved closer to her and put his hand up her ragged skirt and felt for her warm moistness, "Come on then, let's go out around to the back."

He pushed her up against the brick wall at the rear of the pub. Her head was swimmy with ale. She pressed back onto his penetration. Her bony pelvic frame arched forward and back as he thrust. She counted slowly to ten and Mick was spent.

• • •

Tommy woke Molly up in the morning, "Mama, what did you find out about America?"

"Wake your sister and then come sit by me and I'll tell

you."

"What's happened to your arm?"

Molly had a bruise on her right forearm, a souvenir from her encounter with Mick that she needed to explain away to her son, "I slipped and fell walking up the hill last night. It's nothing."

Maureen rubbed her sleepy eyes as they both came to sit on the floor by their mother. Both of the children were redheaded, curly haired, blue eyed, freckle faced beauties. Molly put her arms around them both and hugged them with her words, "With the Good Lord willing, we'll be leaving for America tomorrow."

Tommy jumped up and did jig turns round and round. "Whoopee!"

Molly cautioned, "But I've been told that the ship voyage might be rough. It'll take a long time and some people might get sick and die on board."

Tommy bent down and pulled Maureen up to join him in his dance. He twirled her around and they both shouted, "We're going to America. Whoopee!"

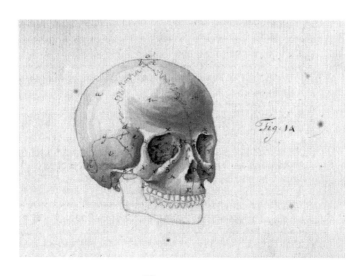

Chapter 11

The Other Body

Augusta, 1854

Sterling had been frozen in place for some time since
John's prank had gone so awry. He muttered to himself,
"What am I supposed to do now with this big dead body
in the alley? John disappeared so quickly. I hope he's all
right, but curse him and his stupid idea for a little fun.
I'll be in so much trouble if anybody finds out about
any of this and so will he. Oh, if the professors find out,
disciplinary action or maybe even expulsion from school.
Now, steady, Strawling. Egad, I miss John already. There's
a lot at stake here. I must think this through and be calm
about it. I am a reasonable man. The porter must have
been on his way to the dissecting lab to take this body for
an anatomy class. I should probably follow through with
that same plan."

The young medical student put two shaky hands on the body and tried to drag it, instantly realizing the impossibility of the task. His mind was racing. *Who can help me, and more importantly, who can I possibly trust at this hour? I could enlist Broom at the boarding house, but I'm not sure I could trust him. He's strong enough, but he'd probably be obliged to tell Mrs. Gardner. There is only one other. It'll have to be Owen. He might be in bed by now, but I can wake him up. I can't think of any favors due me, none that I can call on. But he wouldn't expose John or me. He's our friend, I hope.*

Worrying that the body might be discovered, he began a brisk march back to the house to enlist his colleague. He began to mumble again, "I wonder what's happening to John. I wish this whole miserable ordeal had never happened." As he walked on his mental tone began to change. *John is such a rogue. He seems to get away with a lot. Like the time he broke one of Mrs. Gardner's favorite crystal pieces. He cast aspersions on the slaves. That was a good one. I don't know how he manages it, but he seems to have a string of never-ending good fortune. He might be able to talk his way around the porter.* He tried to mimic John's voice, "Besides, we practically know him." *That's what he said. John's resourceful; he might find a way to escape.* Quickening his pace he queried. "Why, I wonder, that rascal might even beat me back to the house!"

Sterling arrived as the fireplace mantle clock in the front parlor struck eleven. He bolted up the stairs, mindfully avoiding the third and seventh squeaky steps, almost expecting to find John in his room. There was no sign of him, and he angrily threw John's coat and gloves on the bed. Next, Sterling pressed on to Owen's room. Surely Owen would be in his bed. He barged through the door, but Owen wasn't where he was supposed to be either. It didn't appear that he had even been to bed yet.

Sterling could feel his pulse in his ears and his head was beginning to throb. He looked in the study room. There was no sign of anyone, anywhere.

When he came back to the stair landing, he was surprised to see Owen leaning against the railing at the bottom of the stairs. He'd been awakened by Sterling's heavy footsteps and found himself asleep next to Amanda in the best room bed. He didn't want to wake her and he didn't want Sterling to know where he'd been. He had to think quickly.

Owen whispered loudly, "Sterling, what is going on?"

"Where have you been? I've been looking all over for you."

"I was upstairs using the privy, when I thought I heard something, so I came down here to check." In an effort to deflect attention from his own actions, he asked, "Are you home already? Where is John?"

"What? I don't understand how I could have passed without seeing you."

"We must have just missed each other. Has something happened to John?" Owen observed Sterling's frantic behavior as he began his ascent.

Sterling wasn't ready to share all the details of his ordeal, "What makes you ask that?"

"Well, I haven't seen him yet. Did he return with you?"

"Owen, I'm going to need your help."

"What could you possibly need my help with at this hour?" The two young men stood face to face on the top landing. Owen studied Sterling suspiciously. Sterling returned the gaze in kind.

"You're positively rumpled, but your covers are not. What have you been up to?" Realizing the futility of alienating his only possible ally, Sterling changed his tone. "Oh, listen, we're going to have to trust each other. I need your help to move a body."

"What?"

"There is a body in an alley downtown that we need to move."

"What body in what alley?" Owen looked at Sterling skeptically. "This must be one of John's pranks."

Sterling tried not to reveal how close Owen was to the truth for fear he would lose his assistance. "If you'll tuck your shirt in and put your shoes on . . . I'll tell you as we walk. Listen, it's a terrible mess and as much as I hate to get you mixed up in it, I really do need your help."

"Alright, look here, I'm stuffing my shirt in, let's get my coat. My shoes are in the parlor."

"Did you have to take your shoes off to help Mrs. Gardner with her spinning wheel?"

"Sort of," Owen retorted.

"Hmmm...well it seems we're both in a bit of a bind. You're not going to believe this. It was a prank and I'm afraid it's gone terribly sour. First you've got to swear to complete secrecy. Alright?"

"I knew it. Are you going to get us both in trouble?"

"I hope not, but you must swear."

"I will if you will. And if you'll help me study for our anatomy test next week."

"Alright, alright, we'll need to help each other. Besides we may have a better understanding of anatomy when we get done moving this body. Gather your strength. We'll have to get a stretcher or a pushcart from the hospital."

Owen stared at Sterling in disbelief. "But what are we going to do with this body? Where are we going to take it? And what has happened to John? Please tell me, where is he? I don't believe you answered that yet."

Sterling shook his head and stuttered. "I don't know where he is. That's what I've been trying to tell you. John got this crazy idea for a prank. Remember you said that the porter was a resurrectionist? Well, first John wanted to see if he could find a body and then he got the bright idea that he'd trick the porter by making his cadaver disappear." Sterling was relieved he wasn't telling a total lie and continued. "Come on, let's hurry and I'll tell you the whole story as we walk. Let's go and collect a body for our anatomy class."

They both moved stealthily down the steps and into the parlor.

Owen put on his shoes and reluctantly laced them. "Let's go out the back door." He thought there'd be less chance of waking Amanda by going that way.

Sterling agreed without question. As soon as they turned out in the street, Owen asked, "So, am I hearing correctly that John confirmed the porter is a resurrectionist?"

"Well, he definitely had the cadaver we're about to go collect in his bag. There were digging tools in the wagon and I saw some dirt. I'd say there's not much doubt about it." Sterling seemed to be gaining understanding as he explained. He continued relating his version of the story to Owen, adding a few alterations of his own making.

"So, like I said, the idea was simply to take the body out of the bag to play a trick on the porter. John thought he would think his cadaver had come back to life and be completely haunted."

"So you just took the body out of the bag? And then what happened?"

"Well, nothing really. The porter came back to the wagon, but the horse bucked and ran away and the corpse is still in the alley. I guess he'll see it's missing eventually, but I think if we get it back to the anatomy lab, he won't be able to comment."

"Sterling, this isn't making sense. Where did John go?"

Sterling was in deceitful territory, and although he didn't like the way it made him feel, he was hesitant to say anything more about John's being in the wagon or what had really happened. "I don't know. What with all the commotion, we got separated, but I expected to find him back at the house."

"All what commotion?"

"Moving the body."

"So John helped you move the body?"

"Yes, didn't I say that already?"

"Right, but when did you get separated?"

"When the horse bucked and ran away." Sterling wanted the interrogation to stop. He was getting mixed up about the details himself. "And where did you say you were sleeping before I found you in the house?"

"I didn't say I was sleeping."

"Let's concede to allow confusing stories lie still."

"Agreed."

The two medical students found a pushcart outside the city hospital that would serve as a makeshift morgue stretcher. They had to travel two blocks to get to the bank building. As they came into the side alley and viewed the corpse, Sterling noted that the body was still in the same position he left it.

"How in the world did you get this body wedged in here?"

"Trust me; it wasn't easy. Let's see if we can get him out of here."

They moved the cart as close to the fire escape as possible. Dragging the body from behind the fire escape stairs, they rolled the cadaver onto his back. Positioned at each shoulder, they reached under and attempted to lift, but the weight proved too much.

"We've got to find a way to distribute the weight more evenly. Grab under his shoulder and also at his thigh. Don't try to hold him by his shroud. It'll rip." Owen continued. "Bend at the knees."

"We've got to get it this time. What if someone sees us?"

Assisted by adrenaline, they lifted the body enough to get it onto the pushcart.

As they pressed the heavy wheelbarrow through the alley and past Bristow's, it developed a squeaky wheel under the weight.

A shadowy form, with lantern in hand, stood in the doorway as they passed by. "What is it that you men have in your cart there?" It was Mr. King, the barkeeper.

Sterling tugged at his hat to cover his eyes to keep Mr. King from recognizing him from his earlier attendance at the tavern with John.

Owen spoke, "Sir, we are medical students at the college and we were on call at the infirmary tonight when we were told to come down here to see about someone taken violently ill. When we arrived, we found this poor soul stretched out over there in a dark part of the alley."

"This is the first I've heard about any of this." Mr. King walked over to the cart, lifting his lantern.

"Sir, I wouldn't come too near if I were you. We don't know who this man is or what made him sick."

Lamplight provided enough illumination for Mr. King to see the lifeless face of Jacob Brown, the big black man whose body had been disinterred by Grandison Harris. "I don't recognize him either, but he doesn't look sick, he looks dead."

"Yes, sir. That is exactly our conclusion as well. We are merely taking him back to the hospital, so we can attempt to identify him and notify his next of kin."

"On with it, men. Good work. Try to find out what he died from and let me know, will you?"

"Absolutely, sir."

When they were out of Mr. King's earshot, Sterling praised his comrade.

"That was some fast talking and quick thinking, Owen."

"I figured as soon as I said we didn't know what he died of, his curiosity would dampen."

"And right you were."

They pushed the cart through the rutted dirt roads back past City Hospital and on toward the anatomy lab.

"You know, Sterling, a corpse is quite a commodity. I've heard stories of ambulance men in other cities who coax their horses to creep slowly toward the hospital with a critically ill patient. They might even take an extra spin around the block, hoping they'll die en route. If the unfortunate one complies, the driver more than doubles his fare. He takes the body directly to an anatomist to collect his fee. We're not doing anything that sinister. This body was already dead. I wonder if we could collect money for this cadaver."

"Owen, I think you've gone balmy on me. We'll be fortunate if we complete this mission without getting expelled from school. I've certainly had my fill of stories about corpses today."

The streets were motionless. Not even a breeze whispered over their clandestine journey.

"So Sterling, what are your plans to keep us from getting in trouble? What are we to do with the body when we get back to the anatomy lab?" Owen asked.

"You've seen how the bodies are set up in the morning, prepared for dissection. Why don't we put him on the table like that? I don't think it would attract any attention. Look, no one will be the wiser, since he was already sort of scheduled, until the porter got scared and ran off. The porter won't be able to own up to losing the body, lest he lose his job."

"But aren't the cadavers soaked in whiskey before we use them? It lessens the odor and acts as a preservative.

Then I think the porter brings them up from the whiskey vat first thing in the morning. I've heard him mention a keeping room. That's where the whiskey vat must be."

"Owen, are you suggesting that we need to take the body to the keeping room and put the body in the whiskey vat?"

"I'd say so, if you don't want to arouse suspicion."

"That may be the most brilliant idea you've had yet. Now, let me think. So then the porter will go and get this body in the morning from the whiskey vat. That will work. And I'll bet it is going to even be easier to unload the corpse into the vat then to try and arrange him on the table."

Sterling was relieved that Owen was thinking so clearly, until he found a flaw. "But do we know where the special keeping room is?"

"I think I know. It's behind the dissecting wing in back of the stable. Let's look for the wagon and I'll bet it'll be nearby, around back."

Sterling pointed to one of the moonlit buildings, "You think, there? And that appears to be the same buckboard we saw the resurrectionist driving earlier. See the shovel and the ax there? And look at all the dirt." Sterling was also looking for any clues to John's whereabouts.

"I certainly hope the porter has gone to bed for the night and that he is hard of hearing. I wish I had some of that oil I used on Amanda's spinning wheel to quiet this squeak."

"Me too, on all three points. Let's just get on with it."

"We ought to whisper. This lean-to has to be the keeping room."

It was a wooden structure with double doors that were designed to swing open on hinges. "Let's be careful . . . noise." Gingerly they opened one of the doors as quietly as possible. Sterling spoke first, "This is a spooky place."

"I couldn't agree more. It's downright eerie. Let's find some light."

Sterling pointed. "There's a lantern over there."

Owen squinted in the darkness as his eyes fixed on the lamp. It was a metal teakettle shaped camphene lamp filled with its mixture of alcohol and turpentine. He felt for a friction match and its striking sandpaper. He pulled the Lucifer along its flint and held flame to wick. The dark walls illuminated and the two young medical students stood dumbfounded as they stared at the pool of whiskey, a thirty-six inch high rectangular wooden structure ten feet by sixteen feet. At the far end a foot stuck up, looking surreal, like a stationery swan with a comb of toes afloat in a ruddy lake.

"How many bodies do you suppose are in there, Owen?"

"I have no idea, nor do I have any intention of counting."

"Right, let's put this giant in his place.

They moved the cart as close to the reservoir as they could position it. Sterling kept his head turned away from the whiskey pool. "Ugh, the thought of looking in there and seeing all those dead bodies. I'm feeling queasy."

Owen took command, "None of that now. Here, move over a little and help me pick him up. Let's hoist him in there."

"What if we spatter whiskey about?" He looked as nervous as a cat in unfamiliar territory.

"Sterling, are you going to tell me that you're worried about spilling a little whiskey on the floor?"

"No, I guess not. Right…let's heave him then."

Rolling the heavy cadaver from the stretcher over into the vat, with a splash his body hit the golden brown liquid and began its slow descent into three feet of oblivion.

Sterling was about to blow out the lantern.

"Stop, man. Do you want to blow us up? That's a volatile substance in there. Think chemistry."

Sterling used to the brass cap attached by its chain to the lamp to snuff out the flame.

Chapter 12

Digging the Canal

1847

Excavated entirely by hand, it took two hundred workers to complete the first level of the canal. Irishmen, slaves, free blacks and whites comprised the work force that used shovels and pick axes to dig into Augusta's red earth. Companies promoting transportation specialized in building both railroads and waterways. Musgrove's crew broke ground in May of 1845. Graves and O'Brien won the contract on numbered sections eight, nine and ten. Timberlake and Timanus were awarded sections two and three.

The men delving into the clay and granite of section two, farthest down the river and closest to the head gates, had the most scenic section with the wide meandering river rocks poking their tips up to make swirls gush around them. It was a sweltering, muggy July afternoon with the temperature reaching one hundred and three degrees in the scorching sun.

Jess MacNeal was especially hot. He'd drenched through his shirt several times, but now he was dry. Drinking water that didn't seem wet, his lips felt parched and swollen and he was having trouble swallowing. He couldn't remember if it was Monday or Tuesday and his work-mate, Nathan Parker, was making him angry as he swung his steel mattock into its recurring arc of piercing strikes.

"What are you doing there, Nathan?"

"What do you mean, Jess? I'm just swinging the ax trying to break up this clay and rock. Ain't we digging the canal?"

"We're digging a canal? I thought we was doing jail time or something."

"Always the jokester, huh Jess. No, come on now. Shovel that stuff out that I'm hacking at. Didn't you hear the boss man say that the mayor was coming down here today to see how we was doin'?"

"The mayor of what?"

"Jess, now quit that cutting up. You know, the mayor of the city of Augusta."

"Okay," He said with an exhausting sigh. "I'm looking for my shovel."

"It's laying right there. How could you not see it? It's right in front of you. Are you alright?"

"I don't know as I feel so well."

"Well you better make it 'till after the mayor comes."

"Yeah, right" Jess wobbled as he slowly hoisted a shovelful of dirt-encrusted granite up and out of the gully. Dust spat back at him and tan colored dry specks coated his face and tongue. He wobbled again, then dropped his tool and fell over flat on his back in the ditch.

"Jess, what's up with you?"

Nathan looked at his coworker's bluish lips contrasted against his crimson colored face and knew he needed to get help. He looked like he'd been holding his breath longer than anyone Nathan had ever seen. He ran for the foreman, Mark Davis.

As he rounded the corner where Davis was standing he noticed he was in deep conversation with an impressive looking figure. Long gray hair and whitish pointed beard contrasted against his dark black suit. It was the mayor, Doctor Lewis DeSaussure Ford, former dean and still a professor at the Medical College.

Not wanting to interrupt, but knowing that he must, Nathan burst into the middle of the conversation, "Excuse me, sirs, but my work partner fell over in the heat and I think he's bad off."

Ford sprung into action. "Take me to him."

Nathan led the way. As they marched at a quick clip, Doctor Ford slid his jacket from his shoulders and wrestled both arms free. He flung the coat at foreman Davis. When Nathan pointed to Jess' location, Ford jumped down in the trench without regard for the rest of his mayoral attire, put a hand on Jess' searing head and immediately diagnosed, "Sunstroke, I'd say. He's burning up. Help me carry him over to the river. We've got to cool him off immediately."

Davis was following behind. Ford sharply shouted at him, "I'll need some potable water, preferably in some sort of container like a flask, and see if you can find some salt. Bring them to me at the river."

Ford checked to see if Davis understood. He saw a puzzled look. "Drinking water, man, now hurry!"

Nathan grabbed Jess' feet and Ford had his upper torso. The downed digger was a man of medium build, five feet four or so and balding at the top of his head. They walked with him over to shore, a hundred feet away from where they had been digging. The smell of honeysuckle mingled with dried sweat. Jess made a few feeble moaning sounds as he was jostled back and forth toward the water.

"I sure hope he'll make it. He's got a wife with a kid on the way . . . and he's been a good work buddy."

Ford seemed oblivious to Nathan's comments as he commanded the scene and continued barking orders. "Now, take off his boots and socks and slide him down into the water up to his calves. We have to cool him off, but not too fast or he'll seize."

Nathan complied. The river temperature was more than twenty degrees cooler than the air.

Ford reached into his pocket and pulled out a white linen handkerchief. "Do you have some sort of a rag, too?"

"I have this bandanna here around my neck," Nathan untied his neckerchief as Ford unbuttoned the workman's shirt.

The physician took the two pieces of cloth, briefly soaked them in the river water and spread one flat over the man's upper chest. He took the other and placed it lightly over Jess' face.

Nathan was amazed at Doctor Ford's deliberate manner.

Jess was beginning to make more moaning sounds. Davis came back with a canteen of water and a lump of salt. Ford instructed Nathan as if he was one of his medical students. "Every five minutes, we're going to push his body further in the water. We've got to cool him down slowly and get him to drink some fluid. He needs to cool off on the outside and get wetter on the inside. He's lost the chemical balance in his body, so I'm going to make him a salt water solution to drink."

Doctor Ford scraped approximately two tablespoons of the salt into the canteen. He placed the cap on the metal flask and rotated it to mix the solution. He dipped his pinky finger into the brine and tasted. "That'll do."

Jess was more than halfway in the river by now. Ford instructed Nathan, "Help me prop his body up. And what's his name again?"

"Jess is what I've always called him."

The doctor removed the handkerchief from Jess' face, rewet it and pleated it in two-inch folds to place over his forehead, then lifted both eyelids of his patient. "Jess, can you hear me?" The man's pupils quickly constricted to pinpoint size, briskly contracting in the daylight. "That's a good sign, his eyes reacted. Jess, listen to me. I want you to drink some water. It's really important for you to drink now."

More mumblings came from the prostrated man.

"Good, that's good. Now I'm going to pour just a little water in your mouth and I want you to swallow." He lifted the canteen up and turned his head sideways so he could see how much water to pour out. "Come on Jess, swallow that."

He coughed and sputtered and a trickle of water ran down his chin, but he also swallowed.

"That's it. Come on now, again." Doctor Ford patiently repeated the motions. He poured a bigger swig and Jess swallowed it with no choking.

"I think he's almost out of danger."

Nathan and Davis had been quietly watching. Davis spoke first, "He's a lucky fellow. What I mean is; it's a blessing . . . the fact that you happened to be here today. We wouldn't have knowd exactly what to do. Well, we would've knowd to get him out of the sun, but not all this other."

"You really should have safety precautions with set ways of handling certain emergencies. In the middle of summer, on a day as hot as today, it doesn't take long for a man to overheat. I know you men want to get this canal dug quickly, but we don't want anyone to die for it."

Davis listened to Ford's suggestion and thought about continuing his lesson, "Yes sir. Can you tell me why it is that the darkies don't seem to overheat?"

"That's a good question. Their anatomy is different from ours and they tolerate high heat more effortlessly. The effect of Africa perhaps. Let us concentrate on Jess here. Leave him in the water like this until he's fully awake. Make sure he drinks the entire contents of this flask before he moves. After that, see him home, change his clothes and put him into his bed. He'll probably be hungry as a horse by suppertime."

Ford pointed his finger at Jess, "And no more work for you in this heat."

Jess managed a weak, "Thanks, Doc." as Doctor Ford gathered his coat.

Summer progressed and most of the white workers, unable to tolerate the heat, laid down their tools, which were picked up by the Negro workers. Some were slaves and some were freed men.

The first level was completed in eighteen months and on November 26, 1846; the canal filled and flowed according to the engineering predictions. It was seven miles long, five feet deep and forty feet wide at the surface, twenty feet wide at the bottom.

Cotton boats immediately began navigating the waterway. Shallow drafted vessels known as Petersburg boats, with their length of sixty feet and width of seven feet could carry as much as eighteen thousand pounds of cargo, from cotton to household commodities. By June, pleasure boats advertised taking passengers up the canal for a fifty-cent fare.

Following Ford as mayor, Doctor Ignatius Garvin was elected in 1848 as the second and third levels completed the canal's full length to nine miles.

Henry H. Cumming searched for accurate calculations regarding the amount of water needed to operate a given number of spindles in a mill. He requested engineering assistance from George Baldwin, who inspected the canal for two weeks in April 1846. Baldwin's best estimate was that three hundred eighty horsepower could drive a mill with three thousand five hundred eighty-four spindles. He conceded that his mathematics was not based on actual experimentation. Somewhere between approximation and understanding, William Phillips, the canal curator, misinterpreted it to be ten thousand spindles.

Still, without knowing the exact waterpower capabilities of the canal, The Augusta Manufacturing Company, preparing to profit, commenced sale of its stock on January 27, 1847.

Chapter 13

A Voyage

Ireland, 1848

Molly, Tommy and Maureen walked down to the dock at
Galway. It was a three-mile hike from where they had been
living. They had few possessions, and what they did have
rolled into small bundles. The scant sticks of furniture to
which they were accustomed belonged to the landlord.

On arrival at the shipyard, Molly excitedly pointed to the
ship. "Look at her, Tommy. Look at those huge masts and
when they put her sails up, we'll be going across the great
big ocean." Her eyes welled with relieved tears at the sight
of their escape from starvation.

"Mama, could we fall off the ship?" Maureen had a
worried tone in her voice.

"Now, where did you get a fool idea like that?" Molly
looked at Tommy. She cuffed the top of his head. "Have you
been telling your little sister tall tales?"

"Er . . . maybe one or two." Tommy shot a mischievous look at his mother.

"Thomas Patrick McLennan. No more!"

As they approached the gate, they were instructed to stand in the line for the doctor's shop. There was a mandatory health inspection required for clearance before the voyage; a declaration of fitness for travel.

It was a sunny day with a temperature of seventy degrees and Ireland was living up to her Emerald Isle name. Molly fidgeted as she waited. She worried about them passing their physicals. When it was her turn, the Doctor asked Molly to stick out her tongue and he briefly felt her pulse. That was it. She was through the gate; passed with flying colors. So did Tommy and Maureen.

Into another line for what seemed like a long time, but closer to the ship with its empty masts, Molly felt the sun beat on her face. The children didn't seem to mind the wait. She closed her eyes and imagined those beautiful white billowing sails taking her away from her hunger. When she looked up, Mick Kelly was standing in front of her.

"All ready to go, are you?"

"Tommy and Maureen, I'd like you to meet Mick Kelly. He's helping us make this journey."

"Pleased to meet you," were Tommy and Maureen's unison responses accompanied with a little bow and curtsey.

"What charming children."

Tommy kicked his feet in the dirt and gave a devilish look toward his sister.

"Tommy, you're not going to chase me, are you?" Maureen questioned his mischievousness.

Molly started to call out, but Mick took her arm, "Oh, let them run around Love, they'll be cooped up for a long time on that boat. Besides, I wanted to talk to you." He spoke softly and leaned in toward Molly's left ear. "Are you sure

you're up to this? Maybe . . . well . . . what I was thinking
. . . is if you was to stay here, we could see each other
some."

"Mick." She put her right hand up to the side of his
face in a gentle caress. "No, my mind's made up. And you
know how stubborn Irish women can be. I've got to give
these children a chance at a new life. But why don't you
come to join us when you get the opportunity? Come over
to the New World? At least come to collect your money. I
can't tell you how much I appreciate your help."

"I admire your conviction, Molly. I spoke with Father
Callahan and he said to send you his best. He'll call on
St. Christopher to look after your travels and he'll ask the
whole parish to join in with prayers for your safe passage
at Sunday morning mass. Oh, and he told me to tell you
that he believes your husband's sister will also be taking
this ship. You might meet up with her."

Molly moved back from Mick. "Erin Marie McLennan,
well now, fancy that. We haven't kept in touch much since
Corey died. She always went to early services and seeing
me and the kids seemed to be a painful reminder of her
brother's loss."

"Molly, Tommy and Maureen McLennan," the yeoman's
voice called out as he held the ship's roster.

The children came running back to their mother's side
when they heard their names called.

"You've got yourselves a beautiful day to start off." Mick
tipped his hat. "Good voyage to you all. I might be seeing
you, if I get to America."

Molly gave Mick a hug and a peck on his right cheek.
"God bless you, Mick. I'll write you a line or two."

It was their turn to march up the gangway and Molly felt
a swell of pride for herself and her small family. A man at
the top handed out an odd looking yellowish sort of cake.
One issued for all three of them. Molly held it carefully

as they followed the shipman. Down into the steerage compartment they went, through a dark tunnel passage. Her nose reacted to the stench of urine and vomit. She breathed through her mouth to keep from gagging. They emerged into an area where small wooden bunks covered with straw were nailed to the walls. The shipman pointed out three narrow beds in a tiny space. Barely big enough for a child, there would be no room to turn over. Molly looked around at all the berths built into such a small place. She counted only a few other fellow travelers around them, but remembering the line outside, she realized that if all the others were coming to steerage it would be quite crowded.

In her usual manner, she hid her horror from her children. They still seemed optimistic. She said a small prayer, made the sign of the cross and then broke the strange bread cake apart. 'Here, children, have a bite to eat." It was soggy, not quite cooked through, but she handed out equal pieces and they were so hungry, it disappeared.

Twenty more people came, pushing and shoving their way toward their own berths. A sailor began explaining procedures.

"Every family will be issued their rations in the morning along with one-third of a quart of water. The water must be used for both drinking and washing. We have everything meted out. Each family will be issued a pound of rations per adult per day and one-half pound per child. Don't ask for more food. Several chamber pots will be made available and there is one privy over in that corner." He pointed to his far right. "With good weather, this trip will take about a month."

Molly's optimism for the journey was quickly fading. Mick had warned her. She closed her eyes again, this time wondering if she had the strength to endure such a voyage.

She could see that the challenge would require all her courage.

More and more people crammed into their tiny spaces. Tommy quit counting when he passed two hundred. Maureen had fallen asleep on her bed. If this was to be their home for the next month, she'd have to make the best of it.

"Molly, is that you?" a familiar voice shouted. Her sister-in-law was pushing her way forward. "Father Callahan told me you might be here. I've been looking for you.

"Erin Marie, I'm so glad to see you. Did you ever imagine anything like this?"

"Not in my wildest. I heard about Ana's passing. I'm so sorry. Ah, look now, this must be Tommy? Where is Maureen?"

"She's asleep over there. I still can't believe Ana is gone from us. Did Mick book your passage, too?"

"Yes, I think he's booking everyone from our parish. He didn't lead you to believe that he was helping you out of the kindness of his heart, did he? Father Callahan has a fund from donations and collections he gives Mick to use at his discretion. He gets some kind of placement fee from the shippers, so he must be making money. It helps that he's easy on the eyes."

"Really, do you have a thing for him?"

"No, not me. What about you?"

"Well, I can't say that I haven't ever thought about him." Then changing the subject abruptly Molly said, "Mick told me this might be rough, but I had no idea."

"Molly, we need to share the endurance of this voyage together. My bed is just over there a little ways." Erin Marie touched Molly's arm. "I want to spend time with the children, too, and be a proper Auntie. I'm sorry I've wasted so much of that time."

Molly took a searching look at this woman standing in

front of her. She felt as though she'd had blinders over her eyes for a long time, like when a horse has to be led out of a burning barn. As she looked at this sister to her lost husband, she saw a new resemblance, something beyond the McLennan carrot top mop. It was something comforting, some warmth around her blue-gray eyes.

"I'm so pleased that you are here, Erin. This last year and a half has been like hell. When Corey died with his bleeding ulcer, I didn't think it could get any worse. I was wrong about that. I've had days when I just wanted to go on and die . . . get it over with."

"Let's hold onto our hope for a better life. I have a friend. Her name is Theresa Cooke and she arrived in Savannah five months ago. She's sent me several letters. Up the river, she found a job in a new textile mill. There is proper housing, and plenty of food and water. We could go there and find work. We'll simply have to keep looking to the day we can get off this ship."

"Amen."

Molly and Erin counted each twenty-four hour passage. They had a secret place where they made a scratch mark at the end of Molly's berth each night before they bedded down.

Two mornings after they made their first mark, there was a lot of commotion. Someone had been found as a stowaway among the sacks of flour. The captain ordered all the steerage passengers on deck, so that the areas below could be searched. Molly, Erin and the children stayed close together. It was a beautiful morning, blue sky, white puffy clouds overhead, a cool breeze blowing and no land in sight. There was nothing in sight in any direction, but a huge, vast ocean.

The night they made their tenth mark, three people were carried out of the steerage compartment. Dead from typhoid fever was the rumor.

Tommy and Maureen made friends. Freddie Hill was their favorite. For the trip, his parish had donated a homemade checkerboard with white and blue buttons serving as pieces. A special corner with an empty barrel that served as a table was set up for play. There were other children on board, some older, some younger. They all took their turns at the game, but Tommy and Freddie were the champs. The children's resilient attitudes helped the adults tolerate their cramped spaces. Expectant young women dreamed of delivering their babies in the New World. Hope sailed along with them all.

On sunny days, light streamed through the hatchway. Fresh salty air came through there, too, a relief from the staleness. When the hatches had to be battened down because of storms or rough sea, the air became stifling.

Food was meager, but it was better than nothing. Sometimes it seemed as though it was no more than a hardened grain lump with a bit of fat back, but on Sunday there were warm biscuits with a piece of dried beef.

The morning after they'd made their twenty first mark, Molly couldn't get out of bed. She was weak and dizzy. The children were already over at the checker corner, playing. Erin Marie came to attend to her.

"Erin, I must confess, in the middle of the night, way before dawn, I awoke with a terrible pain in my stomach. I arose and went to the privy. There I experienced the most explosive evacuation ever, diarrhea, and since then, I feel so cold. Oh, I'm going to be sick."

"Here, Molly, turn your head this way."

Erin Marie held the chamber pot to the side of her sister-in-law's cot. Molly belched up clear looking fluid laced with what looked like rice grains.

When she spoke her voice was weak and high pitched, "It's the rice water and we both know what that means. Do you see my rosary?"

"Molly, it doesn't always mean cholera. You poor dear, you must be worried sick." She looked for the shiny, crystal set of blessed beads and found them in a rumpled fold of Molly's dress. She placed them in her hands, "Here, darling Molly and say Hail Mary. Will you have a little extra of my water?"

"Erin, I can't keep anything down. What color are my lips?"

"I can't really see. There isn't enough light." But, Erin Marie was afraid to be completely truthful. She could see Molly's lips were as deep blue as the sea they glimpsed weeks ago and her cheeks were beginning to match in color. Her eyes seemed to be sinking into their orbits.

Erin poured some of her water onto a cloth and dabbed at Molly's forehead.

"You don't have to pretend. I know they're blue. We've all heard the tales. I feel so cold. Erin, I want you to promise me you'll take care of the children." She turned her head away momentarily, "My poor children's souls... no father... and now no mother... in a strange new land."

Erin Marie took hold of a shiny bead and shared the religious memento for a moment, "Molly, don't talk like that."

"Erin, promise me . . . I need to know that they'll be cared for."

"Of course I will, but damn this filthy, rotten ship full of its own squalor."

Molly's voice was becoming higher pitched and less audible. "You're so good. Love them for me. Make a life for yourselves. I'm so thirsty."

"Molly . . . wait." Erin Marie called to the children as she put the wet cloth to Molly's lips again. "Tommy, Maureen, come here quickly."

She leaned down to Molly's ear. "Molly, no, please don't go. Not yet. The children are coming. Say your peace to them."

"Oh God, we almost made it, didn't we?"

"We all almost made it."

There was a leaden hue surrounding Molly. It was as though her body was slowly imploding, shrinking and flattening upon itself. Her hands were shriveling and her fingers were drawn together clutching her beloved rosary.

"What's wrong?" Tommy reached his mother first.

"Your mother is very sick. Tommy, say whatever you need to say to her quickly."

"Mother, what's happening? Don't leave us." Maureen was close behind. She stood to the side of her brother with a horrified gaze, mouth open.

In a soprano, barely audible whisper came, "Tommy, be a good boy. Take care of your sister. Your father and I will look after you from above. I love you both."

Molly lay in a motionless state for a time as her effort to breathe diminished and finally ceased.

Burial at sea was simple. Molly's body was wrapped in a white shroud and tied with ropes at the neck, abdomen and ankles. Two other longer ropes lowered her body into the water. Erin, Tommy and Maureen were allowed up on deck to view the ritual, but Erin took them back down to steerage before they glimpsed the line of sharks following the ship.

Tommy couldn't seem to shed a tear. He went back to playing checkers with Freddie.

Maureen buried her head in her mother's old skirt for the rest of the day.

Erin cried her tears in secret. She now had the frightening task of raising her brother's offspring. Moving her belongings to Molly's old bed, she felt the need to be closer to her children.

Chapter 14

Gases

1840 — 1849

A black rubber bladder resembling a thick balloon with a longer neck was being passed from person to person around the room. It was Miss E's turn. A dancer with the ballet, Miss E liked to have fun. As the bladder was handed off to her, she made sure to grab it securely around the neck to keep its precious contents from escaping. She opened the top between index finger and thumb, put the end in her mouth and inhaled deeply. Then reversing her movements, she passed the bag to the person on her right.

Holding her breath while suppressing the urge to hack out the hot pungent taste, her cheeks were filling up with gas and saliva.

"Hold it in, don't start coughing." She heard a command coming from the corner. She began to walk over toward the voice, but she felt more like she was floating. When she reached him, she spewed her breath mixed with spit and the strong, characteristic smell of ether all over his jacket. Then she started to laugh.

Red flowered wallpaper adorned the walls in the room. Miss E couldn't remember the homeowner's names, only that they were rich and she had been invited to the party. She laughed and danced around the room. Up on her bare, strong toes, she pirouetted across the floor bumping into anyone in her way. She lost her balance once, twisted exceptionally around on one leg and touched down on one knee, but quickly recovered to continue her spinning and romping until she backed into the man she'd spat upon. He grabbed her by her elbows and turned her around exclaiming, "Good grief, woman, can't you see where you are dancing?" His eyes glared as he reprimanded her.

She broke away from him, still laughing and waving her hands above her head as he looked down at her left lower leg, "Look, you've bruised your ankle. It is probably sprained. It's swelling and turning purple. Don't you feel any pain?"

Miss E continued to swirl as the young man chased behind her.

"Stop! Will you please stop long enough for me to look at your ankle?"

"Only if you tell me your name," the dancer shouted back at him.

"My name is Crawford Long, young lady. Now stop dancing this instant!"

"Yes, sir," and the young woman crumpled into a pile in front of him.

"I cannot believe you don't feel the slightest pain around this twist," he remarked as he inspected it.

"Are you a doctor or something?"

"As a matter of fact, I am a physician here in New York, training to be a specialist in surgery. I've been to several of these ether frolics before and noticed insensibility. It is quite remarkable, actually. I've seen some people jump over tables and chairs, some made speeches, some became inclined to fight and some wanted to kiss the ladies, but all of them seemed impervious to pain. Does this hurt?" He tested her ankle's range of motion by moving it in a complete circle.

"I don't feel any pain, but I am terribly exhausted at the moment."

He continued pressing on her injured limb in disbelief over her lack of sensation. "This is probably going to continue to swell, so you would do well to elevate it tonight during your sleep. Place several extra pillows at the foot of your bed. Do you have someone to accompany you home?"

"Yes, sir, my friend is over there and we live very near one another. Thank you for your kindness."

Crawford Long believed there was an application for a substance like ether, which could dull sensibilities to such a great extent. He contemplated its use in his surgical practice. The opportunity to test his theory arose some two years later after he had set up his private office in Jefferson, Georgia. Doctor Long was treating a patient, Mr. V, who had a tumor on his neck that required excision.

"I feel that we should remove this cyst. But, I am somewhat concerned about the amount of pain you might experience and I continue to postpone the procedure for that reason alone."

"What are some possibilities of reducing the pain during the surgery?" Mr. V was a curious young man.

"We could load you up on whiskey and morphine. But I wonder, have you ever heard of sulfuric ether?"

"Ether, why yes. Several of the young men in

the county are in the habit of inhaling ether for its exhilarating powers. And I must say that I have inhaled it frequently for that purpose as well. Our common method is to soak a cloth or towel and inhale the fumes. I have become quite fond of it. It makes me giddy."

"If you are familiar with its recreational use and have had no ill effects from it, I would venture that we might attempt its use to remove your tumor."

"I would be most willing to try it."

"We must enlist a witness to verify our events. I will speak with the principal of the academy. He is a good friend and his school is nearby."

On March 30, 1842, Crawford Long positioned Mr. V on his side on his examination table and handed him a towel soaked in ether. Mr. Q, the principal, stood in attendance. Mr. V inhaled the familiar fumes and entered a sleep state where he remained until the operation was over. Doctor Long was able to remove the tumor and when he revived Mr. V, the patient stated he had felt not the slightest pain nor could he believe the tumor was removed until it was shown to him. Long continued to apply his methods, but did not publish his findings immediately as the vehicle he would have submitted them to, the *Southern Medical and Surgical Journal*, had been on hiatus since Milton Antony's death in 1839.

Doctor Long performed other surgeries using sulfuric ether and eventually news of his successful anesthetic experiments reached Augusta. In 1848, Long was invited to lecture to the students at the Medical College of Georgia by Paul F. Eve. Doctor Eve eloquently opened for Doctor Long, "I introduce to you, Doctor Crawford W. Long of Jefferson, whom posterity will honor as the very first man to apply practical anesthesia successfully to surgical operations. He will be crowned as the greatest benefactor to suffering humanity. I greet our guest and congratulate you upon the honor of this acquaintance to a brother doctor for whom the future is bright indeed."

• • •

Six months following, in the winter, Michael J, a student at the Medical College, obtained a quantity of two ounces of ether from a reputable druggist. His motive for use was the exhilarating effects he had experienced on several previous occasions. A twenty-one-year-old, the soon-to-be graduated physician took his handkerchief, poured eighteen drops of the sulfuric ether solution on it and inhaled deeply. Dizziness rushed through his head, his face flushed, and his vision became dim as if he had a thin cloud before his eyes. Hiccoughing and slurred speech followed.

"Oh, this makes me feel like I'm floating. I adore the ringing in my ears."

Several other students were also participating in the festivities, but at a more sensible pace.

Michael J placed several more drops of ether on his cloth, inhaled deeply, and fell back on his bed in lethargy.

His roommate removed the handkerchief, "You've sucked enough of that for the moment."

Michael J became furiously excited and maniacal. He jumped off the bed and ran around the room picking at the air, "I've got to catch these butterflies. Look, aren't they beautiful? Help me catch one." He scooped at the air with both hands as his feet lifted off the floor.

"Michael, there are no butterflies in here."

"Oh, yes there are. Look at them all. There must be fifteen, beautiful, yellow; all fluttering their wings."

Two other students moved Michael J back over to his bed and forced him to lie down. He was soon fast asleep with heavy snoring.

"I'm afraid his tongue is obstructing his throat."

"Wake him up again."

Michael J once again became agitated. Speaking quickly with slurring words and flailing his arms up over his head, "Somebody find me my snot-rag. I need more juice."

"No, Michael, you need to calm down." One of the others doused him with cold water as if he was on fire. "He's starting to scare me."

"It is so cold in here," Michael shivered.

"Come, Michael. We're going to put you back in bed. Here, cover up to keep warm. We'll stay with you until you fall asleep."

Michael J was laughing insensibly, but soon fell into a dull state of drunken stupor from which he did not awake until dawn.

His roommate asked, "How do you feel this morning? I was becoming worried about you last night."

"I have a tremendous pain right in the middle of my forehead, but I know it is Sunday, the fourth of March in the year eighteen-forty-nine."

"Thank goodness your sensibility has returned."

"And thank goodness we have no lectures today. Oh, if only my head would stop pounding," Michael begged.

"Do you want me to call on one of the doctors?"

"Not yet, I'm afraid of their disapproval. They all seem to be teetotalers, if I've heard them correctly, and if they don't approve of alcohol, what would they think of ether?"

"They are physicians and therefore should be non-judgmental. What they choose for themselves is not necessarily what they would impose on others. I think you may need to be seen by one of them. If you insist, we'll give it a while longer before we call on one of them. Speaking of alcohol, why not have a little nip of whiskey?

Maybe that will help your head. Then go back to sleep and we'll see how you feel later."

When Michael J woke up after lunch, his head felt as though it would burst and with his pain superseding censure, a physician was summoned. The previous dean of the Medical College responded.

Doctor Paul Eve, who since his youth had struggled with defects of sight and hearing in the form of myopia and colorblindness, was indeed a teetotaler. He indulged in neither alcohol nor tobacco. But he treated Michael J without prejudice. Magnesia and salts in purgative doses, cold applications to the head, mustard plaster to the neck and warm soaks to the feet with the expression of hope that these means would give entire relief.

Doctors Dugas and Ford were also called in consultation and despite repeated attempts to relieve the pain and reverse his course, Michael J's condition worsened. They attempted every medical intervention they thought prudent. On the morning of the sixth, his symptoms began to mimic spinal meningitis and on the morning of the seventh, Michael J died.

Chapter 15

The Augusta Factory

Augusta, 1850

Rach-a-ta, rach-a-ta, rach-a-ta; that sound multiplied two hundred times composed the din of the shiny green weaving machines' rhythmic clanking. As if they were tapping their toes, the collective cadence shook the floor. Each one was belted to its own power pulley clinging to the ceiling, so it couldn't run away. And in the midst of the orchestration, at each loom, a factory worker wove.

The mill was located at the end of the first level of the canal. It was a brick compound, which consisted of a three-story pickery and a five-story building that housed two hundred looms and five thousand two hundred eighty spindles. It was capable of turning out nine thousand yards of cloth per day.

In the pickery a series of machines loosened and removed any debris still in the cotton. Another set of machinery formed the cleaned cotton into large barrel-shaped rolls called lap. Lap was sent on to the carding room where it was combed into a fine web and drawn through a funnel-shaped device. A larger thick ropelike strand called a sliver emerged. Slivers were later combined, twisted and drawn out into fibers called roving and wound onto bobbins. Spinning on a frame, cotton roving was further drawn out and twisted to create two general types of yarn called warp and weft, which were wound onto different bobbins. Weaving over, under, over, under, combined warp and weft to make cloth.

Two harnesses with cotton thread in suspension moved in opposite directions carrying the warp yarn. An opening was created for a speeding shuttle that ran across the machine, like a mouse being chased by a cat. The shuttle carried the crosswise weft yarn inside the shed. Once the shuttle completed its pass, the reed swung forward and pressed the newest weft yarn tightly and evenly against the already woven cloth to make a new row of weave.

The Augusta factory had been open for nine months, but it still had the smell of new; oil, wood, metal, and rubber blended together. Hints of growing lint balls rested along the baseboards, waiting for more bulk. Tiny worlds of cotton fragments floated by whenever the sun streaked in a window. Humidity was kept high to keep the cotton threads from drying out and breaking.

Textile work was tedious and hazardous. Eleven hours a day, six days a week in a hot, humid building full of lint. The fuzzy air brought on coughing fits. Swiftly moving machine parts might take a limb or sometimes a life. Noise levels were so deafening, it sometimes took hours for hearing to return. The same repetitive motions over and over; empty spindles off, full spindles on. Empty rolls on the loom quickly became full rolls of cloth to load and unload.

To signal the start of the workday, the mill bell clanged from the tallest tower. Workers streamed into the front doors to begin their longer winter hours of work from six-fifteen in the morning until seven-thirty in the evening, including the Irish immigrant McLennans.

Erin Marie worked in the pickery and Tommy was stationed on the main floor with the looms. The two McLennans rarely saw each other during their workday. Erin Marie was prone to worry about Tommy, with him being so young, but the mill manager, Mr. Lucas, said he'd try to get them in the same areas soon. He said it wasn't easy to make out the schedules, but he would do what he could, as soon as he could. He'd promised.

The loom room foreman's name was Pete. He was in charge of all the workers in his area. His job was to walk up and down the narrow rows in between the looms; to make sure things ran smoothly. Pete had a loud deep voice that could project through all the noise, but he'd learned to read lips for the words coming back to him. Lanky and shaped like a beanpole, he stood six feet tall. His coal black hair was dotted with traces of lint and his clothes wore traces of lint, too. He thought it useless to try and keep it off. "Lint head" was a common name for anyone who worked in the textile mill and it was easy to tell who they were.

Tommy started out as a sweeper, moving his broom back and forth swishing up lint and spit. He was a small boy, about three feet tall, able to fit in between the looms and it didn't take much bending for him to fit under them. His pants were starting to shrink up at the ankles and the waist, though. He was eating real food. Meals like beans cooked with a ham bone, cornbread, and collard greens with an occasional potato were served up at the mill lunchroom. Foreman Pete told him he was a quick learner, too, and if he kept up his good sweeping he might get to move up to doffing, where he'd be switching out the spindles.

Tommy still harbored his mischievous streak.

He liked to play pranks on his new friend Bobby, also a sweeper on the day shift. One time he hid Bobby's broom under Mrs. Weston's loom. Foreman Pete had warned Tommy several times that the machinery was dangerous and he shouldn't play around it.

When Tommy swept around Jenny Hill's loom, he saw a big palmetto bug. It was a two-inch long, reddish-brown colored roach, the kind that sometimes took flight. The monstrous insect was hiding by one of the stabilizer pads under the left leg of the machine. Tommy thought Jenny was cute and he wanted to make friends with her, but she wouldn't even talk to him. "Irish" she called him, like it was some sort of disease.

He was going to give her another chance though. Maybe she'd be nice to him today. As he swept around her loom he asked, "Miss Jenny, what sort of cloth are you weaving today?"

"None of your business, Irish," she hollered back at him.

That did it, he thought. She'd had her chance. He couldn't stand the way she talked down to him. He'd get her back for her snotty ways. Tommy stealthily picked up the roach by one of its hairy back legs and moved around behind her. He pulled the collar at the back of her blouse, ever so gently, and dropped in the insect. Then with broom in hand, he shuffled quickly to the other side of the mill floor to sweep behind Mrs. Thompson's loom.

It took a minute for Jenny to start screaming. It was like she'd gotten caught in a machine or something. She screamed bloody murder until Foreman Pete hurried over to see what was wrong. With all the machines flapping together at once, Tommy couldn't hear what was said, but he could see Jenny pointing her fingers in his direction. She was hopping and jumping up and down, flailing her right arm trying to get the bug to move out from under her shirt. She looked funny and Tommy was laughing inside. Foreman Pete got Mrs. Donovan to shut down her machine and accompany Jenny to the water closet to help her remove the bug.

The tall foreman looked around for Tommy and when he spied him, he started after him, stomping his feet with an angry, red face, as if steam might come out of his ears. He swooped down on the boy, like an eagle on a field mouse, lifted him up by the collar and hauled him into the paddling room. Foreman Pete grabbed the largest paddle off the wall and sat down in his chair, pulled Tommy's pants down and threw him over his knee.

"I'm gonna' wear you out, boy. Twenty whacks with this board ought to make you behave. You ought not to able to sit down for a good while neither," he started to smack at Tommy's bare behind.

Tommy bit his lip. He didn't want to let the foreman know it hurt.

Pete had left the door open and several other young workers had gathered outside. "Let that be a lesson to all of y'all. Don't be fooling around on the factory floor. Somebody might get hurt and I don't want no injuries on my watch. We want to practice safety at this mill." He yanked up on Tommy's britches. The other children skittered away from the door.

Tommy stood up and rubbed his bottom, but he didn't say a word.

"Now, go on out there and get back to work," Forman Pete yelled at him. "And don't you even think of not coming to work tomorrow lest you want your pay docked."

Tommy wasn't sure his prank was worth all the fuss. He wished he could become invisible, so everyone would stop staring at him.

Chapter 16

Another Cemetery Visit

1854

"Jacob Brown, it's me, Mary, your woman. I comes to make your spirit rest. I brings the plate, cup, knife and spoon you ate with last 'cause that's supposed to satisfy your soul and keep it from following me back home."

Mary Brown was a tall, gaunt woman dressed in mourning black. A widow of two days, she reached into her sack for more decorations. "And I brings these sea shells for comfort and these bits of colored glass to catch the light and sparkle your spirit. I wants to make sure you're resting comfortably in your sacred spot. You was a good man, Jacob, honest and hardworking. You never gives nobody no trouble. And you being a freedman because your Mammy had been set freed…always having to worry so about doing right. I's glad you ain't suffering' no mores. You's been so sick with your coughing and not able to catch your breath and all that blood you'd been spitting up. What'd Doc call it? Oh, I knows, but I can't remember."

Jacob Brown's intended place of rest was near one of Cedar Grove Cemetery's biggest live oak trees. Its gnarly trunk had been split long ago by a lightning strike and its thick limbs billowed out with short evergreen leaves. Citrus-scented white blooms dotted the stately magnolias. There were a few scattered pines. No fence lined the perimeter of the cemetery.

"And I makes you this memory jug. It's this old green one…It'll collect rain water to soothe you and I's stuck on your old comb and your Mammy's old beaded bracelet and a lock of my hair. I'll adds some more belongings as I find 'em."

Reaching for her last item, Mary pulled out an old quilt. She fanned it open and spread it over the grave and sat along its frayed right edge. "I hope you're not too cold in the ground, but I brings a blanket to warm you, just in case. I's going to sit here and stay with you for a while."

Carefully eyeing other family plots, she noticed that most of the graves had no official markings, but were instead individualized with memorabilia. Families knew where their loved ones were supposed to lie.

She spoke softly to her departed husband. "Jacob, I's got to move in with your brother, Samuel. The rent's not paid seeing as you's been sick for so long. I's gonna' do washing and mending from his place. He says it won't be no trouble. He's a good man, too. I'll get by, though, don't you worry none."

She turned over on her stomach, stretching out on top of his plot and kissed the ground where she believed her husband's body lay, sobbing softly. "I's gonna miss you Jacob."

Turning her head sideways, as though she was nuzzling

against her lover's shoulder, her ear rested near the ground. She quietly held the position for a few minutes, almost dozing off, until she was disturbed by a low soft moaning sound. Startled, she lifted up on her elbows and said, "No Jacob, I needs to know that your spirit's at rest. I's hoping that me telling you about having to move in with Samuel didn't disturb you none. If it's something else . . . if you ain't at peace in there . . . if there's something more I needs to do for you, holler up real loud so as I can hear you and I's go run for help. Let me hear you now!"

Mary put her ear back down on the faded patchwork quilt and listened patiently to the earth beneath it for a long time. She heard no other sound. It was nearly sundown in Cedar Grove.

"Jacob, I ain't heard nothin'. My ears must've been playin' tricks on me. I's got to go home now. Yous knows I can't be in the cemetery after dark on account of restless spirits."

Resolutely, she started her walk back toward home. She began to concentrate on packing for her move in the morning. The smell of early evening cooking fires followed her and the wind, becoming chilled as soon as the sun dipped below the horizon, pushed at her back. Mary loved crisp fall weather. It quickened her step.

Walking into the hallway, she went directly to the hanging mirror and turned it around to face the wall, "Jacob, now, that's just in case your spirit goes floatin' by. I won't want it to reflect and get captured in there, fixin' to haunt me. I've had enough thoughts of haunting for one day."

Chapter 17

Accident in the Factory

1852

Food, shelter, and clothing were the three basic human needs that mill management believed in providing. The philosophy was that satisfied workers produced more than satisfactory work. Erin Marie and Tommy McLennan believed it, too. They were thriving on their mill food, living comfortably in their mill house, and wearing clothing that was manufactured in their mill.

When they landed from their Atlantic voyage four years earlier, Erin Marie moved with the children from Savannah to Augusta. She enlisted her friend, Theresa Cooke, who already worked in the mill to help her find a position. At Theresa's urgings, Erin had placed Maureen in the orphanage for girls. Both women felt strongly that it would be a sin to allow Maureen to work in the mill, when she could receive a proper education. After all, she was an orphan. Tommy agreed. Since he was a boy, they felt differently toward him. He was expected to work and earn his own money. Erin and Tommy visited Maureen almost every Sunday and Theresa would sometimes go along. They all attended Mass in Dublin, a stretch of town between Jackson and Campbell Streets, where most of the city's Irish lived. Sometimes, when the weather was pleasant, they'd all go for picnics by the canal.

Erin Marie and Tommy shared a shotgun house. The house was one room wide, one story tall and several rooms deep with the entrance on the front gable end. If a gun shot through the front door, it could exit the back with no obstruction; hence the name. Theresa lived in one too, two rows back and four doors down. All the mill houses were shotgun-style.

Tommy had done well. He'd gotten more serious about his job and moved up from sweeper to doffer. Occasionally, he even got to help Foreman Pete with a cranky loom that wouldn't work right. He was learning the trade from the ground up. He wanted to know everything about the factory. He wanted to know everything about everything.

Jenny still called him "Irish," but not quite so often or hatefully.

One April afternoon, Tommy was helping Miss Julie with her uncooperative loom. She sat directly in front of Nick Gates and next to Miss Jenny. Tommy had set the brake, but he hadn't cut the power. He thought it was something simple and quick, like a thread tangled up in the motor. He thought he could get it out easily. He got down on the floor and steadying himself with his right hand, he reached up under the loom, putting his left hand in to grab at the threads. As soon as Tommy reached in, Nick instinctively knew something was horribly wrong. He felt like he went into a sort of choreographed slow motion as he set the brake, turned his machine off and moved away from his own loom.

Nick dashed to where the boy sat on the floor. Tommy's face was white and he was unable to speak. Nick grabbed Tommy's left arm and wrapped a lint towel around the three shredded pieces of flesh where his fingers used to be. He wrapped Tommy's hand quickly and tightly, so the boy wouldn't see it. Nick pulled him up off the floor and hurried Tommy over to where Foreman Pete was standing.

Pete said, "What are you doing over here? Get back to your station," but blood was dripping out from under the cloth and Nick pressed Pete to take a closer look.

"We've got to get Tommy over to the hospital, now."

Tommy was woozy and he sank to the floor in front of his foreman. Pete took a piece of strong cotton cord and wrapped it tightly around Tommy's wrist to make a tourniquet. Jenny came over with a wet piece of cloth and began to dab at his forehead. Her action echoed forgiveness for his previous roach attack as she coaxed him, "Tommy, now stay with us. The men is gonna' get you some help. You're gonna' be alright."

"Jenny, please go and tell Mr. Lucas what happened." Pete instructed her to inform the mill manager. "Tell him I'll explain everything when we get back from taking care of Tommy."

Pete got the horse ready for the buggy faster than he'd ever done before, while Nick loaded Tommy into the seat. Pete got in the driver's seat and gave the horse a slap to get her started. They went as fast as they could over to City Hospital.

Once inside, Pete ran to the ward desk and found the supervisor.

"We've got a boy in a buggy outside from the mill who's got a couple of mangled fingers. Is there a doctor who can see him?"

The hospital supervisor instructed the foreman to bring
the boy inside and then went to get Doctor Dugas, who
had completed the surgical theatre for the day and was
looking in on several of his post operative cases.

John Wilkinson, Jr. was spending the summer as
Doctor Dugas' apprentice.

"Let's take him into the treatment room where our
instruments are located." Dugas led the way. Tommy
was half conscious and Pete was carrying him down the
hallway. He placed the boy on the stretcher and then
excused himself.

"I'll just be waiting outside. His name is Tommy
McLennan. And I'd appreciate any news you can give me
so I will know what to tell his Auntie."

"Yes, we will inform you when we have finished. One
question, do you know if he's right or left-handed?"

Pete anxiously answered, "Sir, I believe he's right-
handed. I warned him about those machines." The
foreman shook his head as he left the room.

Doctor Dugas spoke reassuringly. "Can you hear me,
Tommy? We're going to take a look at your fingers and
see what we can do for them. But first we're going to put
your hand on ice to numb it. And we'll give you a little
something to make you sleepy."

"Yes, sir."

"I didn't believe in gases for a long time, as I preferred
mesmerism." Doctor Dugas lowered his voice to speak
only to John. "Some patients seemed resistant to the
trance and gases have almost become routine. Yet, there
is still another alternative. I believe there are applications
for local types of numbing, such as for amputation of
fingers or toes. Now it's not just a simple matter of
choosing between chloroform and ether. It is amazing
how we make progress in medicine."

"So this is ice and salt that we are using?"

"That's correct, John. Start to take that bandage off, but for the moment leave the tourniquet alone. Tommy, can you feel anything?"

"No, sir

"Good, now we want you to drink this medicine." John helped steady a small glass with tincture of laudanum, while Tommy sipped it.

"You let us know if you can feel anything, Tommy."

"We'll need to probe the wound. I would imagine coming from the mill, that his wound will be jagged and dirty. Let's add some tar water to the ice for its antiseptic qualities."

John felt a little squeamish when he saw Tommy's ripped fingers. The index finger showed bone intact and skin on the right side. The skin on the left side of his finger was hanging loosely, but seemed to be in one whole piece. His middle and third fingers were missing bone, and the remaining skin resembled chewed meat. His little finger and thumb were unharmed. John added tar water to the ice and salt soaking mixture in the pan as instructed.

"Now untie the tourniquet at the wrist."

"Yes, sir."

"He's fortunate to be right handed, with this happening to his left. From looking at this, what would you say we'd need to do, John?"

"It looks to me as if the index finger may be saved with stitches. The second and third are nearly gone, so cleanly amputate to stumps?"

"Excellent, that's exactly what I'd say. I'll do the cutting. Do you want to try your hand at the stitching?"

"Yes, sir, I would. He seems to be oblivious to pain presently."

"That's a blessing, too."

Doctor Dugas disarticulated the remaining bone in

Tommy's fingers and neatly cut the skin so it could be sewn cleanly.

John had a needle threaded with suture and began to sew the stitches as Doctor Dugas taught him. "Pulling the stitch through the skin feels different than when I was practicing on that pillow. It's harder to push. But making the knots is the same."

"You are doing an excellent job. Now, I would add another one here."

"We'll have to hope that it doesn't go to pus. The wound looks amazingly clean, considering the machinery involved."

"Right you are. You're almost finished. Two or three more stitches and he's becoming less sedate."

John spoke with a soothing tone, "Tommy, we are almost done here. Hold quite still for several more minutes."

"There, now what sort of dressing would you apply?"

"A lint one, stuffed down over the two lost fingers and then wrapped around the hand like a mitt."

"You are having a banner day here, John. I'm not sure you even require an instructor."

"No, Doctor Dugas, I am learning so much from your tutelage and I am certainly appreciative, sir."

"Very good then, and our little patient is doing quite well."

"Here, Tommy, sit up slowly. How do you feel?"

Groggily the boy asked, "What's happened? My hand is bandaged."

"Let's go out here to talk with the men who brought you to us."

John carried Tommy out to the anteroom where Pete and Nick were waiting.

"Here he is. And he's all patched up." Doctor Dugas pointed to his own hand. "Tommy, look at my hand.

You've lost these two fingers, but the rest of you will be fine. John and I will monitor your progress. We'll change your bandage and check your hand every other day. Don't take the bandage off or get it wet. No work for a while either." He handed a small vial to Pete. "Please give this to his caretaker. It's for pain. Five drops of this laudanum mixed with some tea every four to six hours should keep him comfortable."

"Thank you, doctors," Pete and Nick recited in unison.

They carried Tommy back to the buggy and took him back to the mill house he shared with Erin Marie. She was home, waiting for Tommy, having been told of his injury by Mrs. Donovan. Work production slowed with the foreman away for the afternoon.

Erin Marie hugged the boy lovingly when he came in and Pete gave her the vial of pain reliever, reciting Doctor Dugas' instructions.

"Aunt Erin, I just want to go to my room and lay down."

"Is your hand hurting you any?"

"Not now, I feel sleepy. I met two nice doctors, though. I might want to be a doctor someday."

"Keep up that dreaming, Tommy boy. I'll get you an extra blanket for the bed."

Erin tucked Tommy into his bed and then went back out to talk to Pete and Nick.

"I can't thank you enough for what you've done for Tommy today."

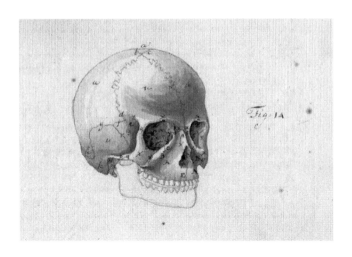

Chapter 18

Cadavers

George Madison Newton had been dean of the Medical College since 1844. With his hairline receding to the top of his head, his sandy-colored curls cascaded down to his earlobes. Softly arched eyebrows rounded over his dark eyes. Closed lips revealed the upper protruding slightly over the lower. He stood at the head of the table surrounded by six other faculty members, ready to address them.

He cleared his throat as a call to order. "Gentlemen, I have requested this faculty meeting to discuss a serious situation among us. I will speak directly to the problem. For years we have had varying methods of attaining adequate numbers of subjects for our anatomy courses. All our previous methods are at challenge. I am sure we all agree that in order to pursue the study of medicine, the dead must be examined to benefit the living. We must investigate a more reliable system for cadaver procurement. However, with dissection still being considered a penal offense, we must be extraordinarily prudent. As long as we act with discretion and acquire our subjects invisibility, we may be able to continue our courses, particularly and especially if we continue with our good deeds within the community such as we accomplish with our dispensary." Dr. Newton rose and stood behind his chair. "Our student body is increasing in number and we have a duty to provide them with the best medical education in the South. In sheer volume we require at least sixteen subjects per term. Mr. Clegg has never overcharged us, but he has become somewhat undependable. I understand that, over the years, he has had drunken excursions and they continue. We certainly cannot afford to bring an embarrassment to our ranks. Costs have been increasing. We've had to pay upwards of ten dollars each to bring subjects in from out of town. Once, we had to authorize forty dollars for a specimen from Savannah. Of course, we are not alone in this struggle. With new medical schools emerging, there will be even more demand for cadavers to supply the demonstration of anatomy. We must formulate a new strategy, and yet still remain sensitive to our local community."

"Didn't we purchase a large number of subjects from up North several years ago? Baltimore or New York, wasn't it?" The voice came from Louis Alexander Dugas. He was enjoying his new position as Chairman of Surgery, which he inherited upon the resignation of Doctor Paul Fitzgerald Eve. In 1850, Eve accepted a position in the medical school at the University of Louisville. Prior to leaving, he was credited as the first American surgeon to perform a hysterectomy.

Doctor Dugas was working on developing diagnostic signs for dislocated shoulder joints. He had animated, dark, wide-set eyes, broad forehead and dimpled pointed chin, which seemed to nestle into his upturned shirt collar, brimmed by a black cravat. He appeared younger than his forty-eight years.

All of the physicians associated with the Medical College continued as medical leaders in their specialties; innovators in new treatments and therapies.

Joseph Adams Eve, the kind-hearted deliverer of babies, shaped generations of Southern physicians with his lectures and papers. He came to be called the oldest teacher of obstetrics in the world and he also fathered eleven children of his own.

Fifty-one year old Lewis DeSaussure Ford drummed his fingers on the table. "I agree we need some sort of strategy change." After his stint in city government, he was selected as the first president of the Medical Association of the State of Georgia. He was also instrumental in the discovery of quinine in the treatment of malaria and served on the faculty for over fifty years.

In 1847, one year prior to succeeding Ford as the mayor of Augusta, Doctor Ignatius Poultney Garvin attended a convention in Philadelphia that laid the foundation for the American Medical Association. He maintained an active political presence and he also inherited the editing of the *Southern Medical and Surgical Journal* along with Doctor Dugas. It continued to be published monthly, after being revived in 1845, with each ambitious issue containing roughly sixty-five pages.

These men of science were well traveled, sophisticated and serious about their practice of medicine and research. They were involved with the development of medical associations both locally and nationally and they continued in their civic duties as well as their public health endeavors.

Doctor Newton continued, "Buying cadavers from

the North and shipping them down here is fraught with difficulties. Not only is it expensive, but the passage is perilous. It would not be a suitable long-term solution. I have another thought, but it will need all of your approvals."

Henry Fraser Campbell, the newest member of the faculty, spoke up. "We certainly do not want to be compared with the Thomsonians... those charlatans with their herbal medicines. Their ranks seem to be incessantly increasing. Continuing to validate our scientific methods with thorough investigation is imperative. We must find a way to obtain sufficient specimens to continue to educate our medical students." Credited with cataloguing the autonomic nervous system in his writing "The System of Nerves," he was a hefty twenty-eight year old with bushy eyebrows and beard. Henry and his brother, Robert, were sons of Mary Eve Campbell, the sister of Joseph Adams Eve. They were to become pioneers in preventative medicine. Campbell began pacing around the others seated at the table.

There was unanimous agreement in the room that something had to be done about the lack of cadavers as learning materials for the medical students.

"What do you propose then?" Doctor Alexander Means spoke up for the first time. Serving as Professor of Chemistry and Pharmacy, he enthralled students with his predictive powers, foretelling the inventions of electricity, telephones and automobiles.

Doctor Newton responded, "I propose that we each contribute one hundred dollars and with that sum in hand, one of us travel to Charleston to purchase the healthiest male slave that can be had for that amount of money. He can work here with us as a porter, but his main function will be to procure the specimens we need to continue our anatomy lectures."

Campbell stopped pacing and raised an eyebrow at Newton. "Am I to understand that we are speaking of entering exclusively into the grave robbing business? If so, how will we be able to remain sensitive to the needs of the community while we do that?" Although he was an 1842 graduate of the Medical College, he seemed oblivious to the methods of cadaver procurement. He had recently been given the first salaried faculty position, a newly created title of "Chairman of Comparative and Microscopic Anatomy." His yearly stipend amounted to five hundred dollars.

Ford responded, "Cedar Grove Cemetery has been a source of supply in the past. Now it must be our main source. Our need for cadavers will continue to increase in direct correlation to our student population. If we could methodically teach a fellow how to dig up a fresh gravesite, extract a body and put it all back together so that it looked undisturbed, I think it might provide a solution as an end to justify our means."

Campbell retorted, "Let me be the devil's advocate for a moment. And you think someone could do that numerous times and in such a manner as to remain undiscovered?"

Newton answered, "As Doctor Ford suggested, if we taught him properly and he was prudent, he could maneuver undetected for a long time. He'd have to do his work at night. Most folks know that a Negro would never set foot in a cemetery at night. We might even teach him to read and write. May I entertain a motion?"

Following Robert's Rules of Order, Doctor Ford raised his hand, "I make a motion that we each contribute one hundred dollars to a fund that will enable us to purchase a slave to assist with necessary duties here at the school. And I'll add that Doctor Newton should be the one to carry out the transaction."

"Second!"

Doctor Newton acknowledged, "And here is a second, duly noted, by Doctor Means. All those in favor?"

Unanimous ayes went round the table. Doctor Campbell dispensed with his objections and decided to see how the plan came to fruition.

"I will expect your contributions by the end of the week and I will make inquiries regarding the necessary arrangements."

And so it was decided that George Madison Newton, hailed as the first full-time faculty member, an excellent instructor and a man completely devoted to his profession, should travel to Charleston, South Carolina. He would carry a coffer of seven hundred dollars, amounting to a one hundred dollar contribution from each faculty member, to solve their specimen problem.

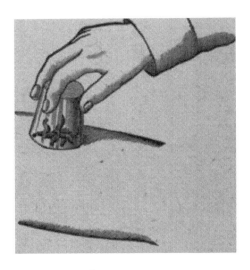

Chapter 19

Bloodsuckers

John Wilkinson, Jr. carefully carried a small jar in one hand and a sack containing dressing change material in the other as he made the two-mile trek over to the mill community. When the houses began to look alike; same size, shape and clapboard siding the color of grayish brown drab, he began to count. Third house from the corner of Gracie Street on the left, were his instructions.

He turned up the walkway and gingerly set the jar down with its slimy, precious cargo to free his hand for knocking. The front door opened with Erin Marie at the other side. John was making a post-operative house call to Tommy two days after his injury. Erin Marie was encouraged by mill management to stay home and care for her nephew.

"Good morning, ma'am. Am I at the right house? I'm here to see Tommy McLennan."

"Yes, this is certainly the right house. Are you Mister

Doctor John, as Tommy calls you?"

"That seems to be the name he has christened me with, doesn't it?"

"Yes, I am his Auntie, Erin Marie McLennan. I am pleased to meet you."

"Miss Erin Marie McLennan, I am pleased to meet you as well. I am John Wilkinson, apprentice to Doctor Dugas and planning to soon enroll in medical school."

"Won't you come in, please?"

"Yes. Thank you. I will need to see our young patient." He bent down and retrieved the jar. "How is Tommy progressing?"

"He's been sleeping quite a lot, but when he is awake he seems to be quite well. He complains of a little discomfort, and I've been giving him the medicine that was prescribed . . . in his tea."

"Good, the medicine is making him sleepy, as it should."

"What have you got there in your jar?"

"Probably better if you don't ask."

"Really?" Erin Marie pouted, slightly offended at his response. She wanted to know everything involving Tommy's care and she hoped to be encouraging to his interest in medicine.

John read her face, "Alright, then, if you really want to know, these are leeches. I'm going to place the little buggers on Tommy's wounds to bleed them and keep them clean. They'll stave off the pus."

"Oh, you were correct . . . sorry . . . I wish I hadn't asked."

John light heartedly said, "I didn't think you'd want to know."

"Would you like some tea?"

"That would be nice, if it's not too much trouble."

"No trouble at all. I'll just put the kettle on to boil.

Tommy is in the bedroom there." Erin pointed to the right side of the hallway.

John tiptoed over to the doorway and peered into his room, "He does appear to be sound asleep."

"I'm not surprised. Come and have your tea first, then."

"I don't mind if I do."

Erin Marie bent down and peered into the jar John had left on the table. "Will those leeches hurt him?"

"No, I've been told to say that it feels more like a tickle. I thought Tommy might find it fascinating . . . to be able to watch them, I mean. Boy stuff, you know?"

"Ah, yes, I know. My brother, God rest his soul, used to play with frogs. He teased me with them. Once he put one in my bed as a joke. Yes, I know something about little boy stuff. Poor Tommy hasn't had much of an opportunity to be a boy. He's had to work more than he's had time to play and he's been no stranger to hardships in his short life."

"He's had other hardships besides losing two of his fingers?"

"Oh my, yes. Back in Ireland, he lost his father. His father was my brother. His baby sister died in the famine and then his mother died on our voyage to America."

"I'm sorry to hear that."

"He's a tough lad, though . . . bright, and he has the spirit."

"I'll say." John paused and looked at this woman sitting in front of him. She was pretty, and petite with flaming red hair, freckles and green eyes. He found her voice and Celtic speech intriguing; strangely soothing.

"Do you have to do anything to the leeches before you use them?"

"Why, Miss McLennan, if I didn't know better, I'd say you're fascinated with them, too." John's blue eyes sparkled with amusement. "Yes, I will need to take them out of the jar and dry them off. That seems to make them suck better and I'll use a new technique that Doctor Dugas and I recently read about. You'll see."

Erin Marie had felt John's stare. She caught her breath as she found the man sitting across from her too handsome to describe with words.

Tommy appeared in his doorway wearing his nightshirt. His hair was tousled. "Howdy to Mister, Doctor John."

"Hello, Tommy, glad to see you've finally awakened. How are you feeling?"

"Fairly well."

"Good, then come over to the table. We have a project to perform."

"What is that?"

"We're going to put leeches on your wounds and let them suck."

Tommy spied the jar and peered into it, "Wonderful!"

"Let me remove the dressing on your hand and let's begin."

"Doctor John says it doesn't hurt at all," Erin added.

John began uncovering the sutured stumps on Tommy's hand where his fingers had been. He studied the young boy's face as he realized it would be his first viewing of his newly rearranged appendage. Tommy acted as though he was a distant viewer, an astronomer peering though a telescope, waiting for stars to collide.

John proceeded. He took one of the leeches out of the jar using a small pair of clamps. In a firm but gentle grasp, he showed his young patient the speckled underbelly of the medicinal bloodsucker. It was an inch long with a cylindrical flattened body decorated with six brown stripes on its backside and it was segmented, like its distant relative, the earthworm. Five tiny pair of eyes and a disk shaped sucker distinguished its front end. John explained that the leech would leave a Y-shaped mark where its three jaws had done the work of cleaning Tommy's wounds.

The physician apprentice placed the animal directly on top of what remained of the boy's middle digit.

John explained as he worked. "If I place this cupping glass with its suction bulb and gently squeeze to create a vacuum, the bloodsucker's own air supply will be exhausted and he'll latch onto the tissue more firmly."

Tommy and Erin Marie were intently watching as John's diligence proved successful.

"Look, the cupping glass worked. See how he's taken hold? Our old method was to put a little sugar over the wound to make them latch on."

"It feels prickly."

"But it doesn't hurt, does it?

"No, it just feels odd."

He placed another leech at Tommy's other finger amputation site and repeated his procedure. Within fifteen minutes, the tiny vampires drank their fill, became distended with blood and fell off. John placed them both back in his jar and began to redress Tommy's wounds.

"How is it, Tommy boy?"

"Alright, but I've become tired again."

"Back to bed with you then," Erin stood up and assisted her small charge back to his mattress.

"Please bring him back to the hospital, day after tomorrow. Doctor Dugas and I will have another look at his hand then. And congratulations on taking such good care of our patient." John stood up, preparing to leave.

Erin's cheeks flushed, "Same to you, sir, for all the work you did today. Thank you for taking such good care of him." Erin hugged him.

John flustered at the unaccustomed affection, "Miss McLennan, it's the least I can do."

"Call me Erin, please."

It was John's turn to blush as he left the shotgun mill house.

Chapter 20

Stranger Than Truth

Doctor Alexander Means was an Irishman and a chemist. He had a reputation for presenting fascinating lectures. He was also known for dispensing with formalities and would sometimes simply relate odd tales in a show-and-tell fashion. With his engaging and animated manner, he held the students hostage as they anxiously listened to hear his unfolding tales. Doctor Dugas had encouraged John to attend one of his afternoon discourses.

Means entered the classroom embracing rectangular objects in each arm.

They were both draped with material to add an air of mystery.

"Today I'm going to relate two very different case histories from colleagues of mine. The first is from a country doctor who attended to Mr. R, a healthy farmer, age of fifty, who had been under his care for two years for occasional severe nervous symptoms. During the first year, irregular sudden attacks of insensibility occurred. Mr. R would fall and sometimes lose consciousness for several hours at a time. Afterward he would seem to recover completely. There seemed to be no set pattern to his attacks. They were separated by weeks or even as much as a month of seemingly perfect health. During the second year, Mr. R's condition seemed to worsen as his attacks progressed toward epileptic fits, occasionally occurring several times in one day. A severe headache or stomach upset would often follow and last for several hours. He did not complain of these symptoms at any other time, but only immediately following an episode. Between attacks he seemed in excellent health. There continued to be no pattern of predictability. The doctor repeatedly purged his patient with cathartics with little result. Mr. R never vomited until one evening after dinner. Having finished a meal of fresh pork, he became quite distressed in his stomach. No seizure was experienced, but strangulation began to occur. He regurgitated his entire meal along with this."

Doctor Means reached into one of the draped boxes and pulled out a three inch red lizard that he dangled by its tail. He then removed the cover and placed it on display in its small glass aquarium. "The lizard is living and appears to be well. Feel free to pay your respects later," he said dryly. "Since that time the patient has returned to perfect health, much like the lizard. There have been no other episodes, no seizure activity, no unusual sensations or pains in the head or the stomach. He did remember that sometime before he began to suffer with ill health, on a day when he was drinking fresh water at the spring, he felt that he might have swallowed some small lumpy substance. Having forgotten about it until he saw the lizard, he now believes this is how he came to share his stomach with the creature. It does appear from this example that an animal can exist in a man's stomach for a period of time. In this case we estimate the lizard coexisted with Mr. R for some twenty-eight months."

Doctor Means surveyed his classroom.

"On a completely separate note, who can tell me the latest advance in cod liver oil?" He also insisted on class participation.

All of the students came to attention at his question, but no hands rose in the air.

"Has no one read the recent edition of the *Southern Medical Surgical Journal?* I would remind you all of the imperativeness of remaining current within your profession by reading periodicals."

John shyly raised his hand. He feared retribution from students more his senior, since he was only an apprentice.

"Yes, sir, you there, what say you?"

"There is a new taste being added to cod liver oil. Preparation of the more palatable mixture is occurring in Italy. It is sardine flavoring that is described as a pleasant sensation on the tongue and is suggested to be served over hot toast."

Doctor Means congratulated, "That is it, exactly. Now class, doesn't that sound delectable?"

Several moans were audible from the audience.

"Our next case study is about the use of electricity. Look at this!" As if a magician, he lifted the cover with a flamboyant flair. "From the city of New York, it is one of Doctor S. B. Smith's Torpedo Magnetic Machines."

Doctor Means had borrowed the promising apparatus and brought it to class. It was the shape and size of a cigar box. The top half was painted with a picture of Doctor Smith's downtown storefront office in New York City. The bottom cavity held a battery consisting of zinc with a copper insert. Doctor Means was interested in the applications of electricity's curative powers. He believed neuralgic pains and certain types of paralytic afflictions could be treated with an electro-magnet. Doctor S. B. Smith claimed that treatment with his Torpedo Magnetic Machine could cure any malady.

Doctor Means pointed to the box. "One and one-half volts can be generated by the battery when copper sulfate solution is poured into this trough. The voltage spins a small electric motor, which acts as a step-up transformer and increases the voltage high enough to give electric shocks. The intensity of the shock can be regulated by sliding this metal bar up into the center of this coil. The farther the bar is slid into the coil, the greater the magnetic induction and therefore, the greater the shock. Patients can either hold onto these two electrodes with their hands or have them applied to various affected body parts, by their physician."

Doctor Means continued, "Another of my physician friends practicing out in Washington County was attending to a Negro slave who had rheumatism in his left vastus externus muscle. And where is that class?"

From the back of the room, a voice answered, "It's the largest muscle in the thigh."

"Thank you. I'll refer to the slave by the letter M. M also had arthritic pains in his right ankle, which displayed a considerable amount of swelling. My friend placed his patient on a long table and positioned the electric poles. He aligned the negative pole over the sacral area at the lower end of his spine and the positive pole was held over the affected ankle. A certain amount of electricity was applied to the body part for approximately one hour. According to M, it felt slightly numb, but there was no twitching evidenced in the extremity. The next morning the physician returned to find that the swelling in the ankle had completely disappeared along with M's discomforts. He no longer had pains in any part of his body. For good measure the physician applied the poles for one more treatment. It has been reported that M has been well ever since. Moral for today is to keep an open mind as you go into your practice of medicine. If there are no questions, class is dismissed…Oh, but don't forget to look at the lizard on your way out."

Chapter 21

Tommy Three Fingers

Tommy's hand was progressively recovering with no sign of infection and the healers were pleased with their handiwork. John removed the stitches on the fifth day and since a bandage was no longer necessary, the young patient was being discharged from routine visits, only to be seen again if a problem developed.

"Mister Doctor John, I want to become a doctor just like you when I grow up."

"Why Tommy, that's flattering. Thank you. How old are you now? Twelve?"

"I'll be thirteen next month."

"I wish you an early happy birthday, then."

"Thank you. The mill is offering reading classes and I'll be signing up soon. Do you think if I study real hard, I might be able to be a doctor like you someday?"

"I don't know, Tommy. It depends on how much work you're willing to do. I sense that you're a determined young man, but it takes more than just determination; school is important too. After you learn to read and write, do you think you could go to school?"

"I don't know Mister Doctor. We're still poor, but we're better off than we were."

"Tommy, your Auntie told me that your mother died on your voyage here. If you don't mind my asking, what happened to her?"

"Have you ever heard of a coffin ship?"

"No, I don't believe I have."

"I've heard Auntie Erin call it that. It's the kind of ship they put us Irish on to come over to the New World. They stuffed us all into tiny spaces like coffins and lots of people died of diseases. My mother was one."

"I'm sorry to hear that. But you knew your mother?"

"Oh, yes. She's only been gone four years now. When my baby sister died of hunger, my mother made up her mind that we were going to have a chance at another way of life. She was determined."

"It's good you knew her. I never got the chance to meet mine. She died while she was giving life to me."

"Is that why you wanted to be a doctor?"

"It is certainly one of the reasons."

"We both have reasons to be doctors, don't we?"

Doctor Dugas came into the room. "Let's see this hand of yours, Tommy. Did John get you all fixed up?" He took the boy's hand and turned it from side to side, examining it closely.

"Yes sir. He took my stitches out and said I don't need to come back unless something bad happens."

"It does look fine. It'll take you a while to learn to do things in a new way, what with those two fingers missing, so be patient with yourself. And if you don't think you can hold something at work, let your boss-man know before you try too hard and hurt yourself."

"I guess they can call me 'Tommy missing two fingers.' I told Mister Doctor John that I'm gonna' be learning to read and write. He says if I can go to school maybe I can be a doctor some day, too. I'd sure like that."

"Really?"

John felt tension in Doctor Dugas' question. He changed the subject, "Why don't we call you Tommy Three Fingers?"

"That does sound better."

Doctor Dugas dismissed the boy, "Run along now. And mind those machines. Treat them with respect for the damage they can do. We don't want to see you injured again."

"Yes, sir. Me neither. Thank you."

Tommy ran out to find Erin Marie to show her his hand without its bandage. Her head was peering around Tommy, desperate for a glimpse of John.

"I guess we'll all get used to looking at your hand like that soon enough." She feared her disappointment was showing. "I'm really sorry that you had such a bad accident."

"Mister Doctor John called me Tommy Three Fingers."

"You saw him then?"

"Yes. He said if I study real hard and go to school, I might be a doctor like him someday."

"He said what?"

"Come on, Auntie, let's go home. I've got to learn how to read." Tommy took Erin Marie by the hand and tugged her out of the building.

John was stuck in the hospital in the grips of Doctor Dugas. "Did you really encourage him? Did you really tell him that he could become a doctor someday if he went to school?"

"Well, not exactly in that manner, but he is a bright boy. I wanted to offer him some hope. He was so excited.

He's such a resolute little fellow, and he's had a rough time of it."

"It's probably best not to encourage a mill youngster. And aren't they Irish folk, from a completely different social class? Unless he had a seriously dedicated mentor, it might be too big a disappointment for him."

John felt a sense of dejection, but he understood the implications of his tutor's words.

It was a beautiful spring day in the city of Augusta. Erin Marie tried to stop thinking about John. She admonished herself for her attraction toward him. She pushed her fantasies away. He was a dedicated young doctor in training and he cared for his young patient, her nephew. Still, she had hoped. Jolting herself, she knew that she needed to stop her daydreaming and face reality. Millwork was awaiting Erin and Tommy's return. They were doing ever so much better than starving in Ireland.

As they walked through the downtown, the dogwood trees and azaleas were in full bloom. Pink and white flowers popped out in vibrant contrast to their green backgrounds. Scattered purple flowery cones of wisteria sweetened the air and bluebirds scratched at the ground in the warm sunshine, searching for nest-building materials.

From a block away, Erin could make out the figure of a man sitting on the front step of their house. Her hope that it might be Doctor John, who had somehow miraculously, beat them to the house, faded as she came closer and noted a heftier build and workman's clothing. Gray strands of hair added years to his appearance, but she'd never forget him. It was Mick Kelly.

Erin Marie ran up to greet their visitor. "Mick, I don't believe my eyes. Is that you? How in the world are you and what are you doing here?"

Tommy stayed at the edge of the street with his feet

planted firmly, his arms folded over his chest in an angry stance.

"Yes, it's me," said Mick. "I've gotten a job here in America, on the railroads. My crew is assigned to survey for a railroad connector spanning the Savannah. We're stationed across the river in Hamburg. I'd heard that you ended up working here at the Augusta Factory." In a louder tone, so Tommy could hear, Mick said, "And I heard about Molly. I'm real sorry about it all. That's why I stopped working for the shippers. I couldn't bear the thought of sending people on boats where they might die. I knew it was bad and I tried to warn her, but she wanted to take her chances . . . no different from you. I guess I held out hope that it wasn't so terrible. At least I didn't want it to be."

Tommy ran up the sidewalk and made a fist with his right hand. He put his left hand behind his back to protect it. He took a full swing at Mick, hitting him in the stomach, "You killed her. You killed my mother."

"Whoa, Tommy Boy, hold on. I cared for you mother, too. I didn't want no harm to come to her. I swear, I would've never done nothing to hurt Molly." From behind, Mick grabbed Tommy around the waist and held him in a bear hug.

"Be careful with him," Erin Marie screamed.

"I'm just trying to keep him from hitting me again." He turned the boy around to face him, pulling both elbows out from his grip. As Mick silenced Tommy's hands together in prayer posture, he glimpsed his left hand.

"Good God, what's happened to you?"

Erin answered, "We've had a bit of a rough time, Mick. Tommy had an accident in the mill last week." She gently pulled the boy's arms from Mick's grasp. "Wait here a while, I'll be back."

Tommy was crying loudly, "She's dead and it's all your

fault!"

"Come on Tommy, let's go in the house. I'll make you a cup of tea. I know you miss your mum. I miss her too." Tommy kept sobbing.

Erin stroked his hair with calm deliberation as he drank his tea laced with pain reliever until his head drowsily nodded. She helped him into bed. When Tommy was settled and asleep, she came back to the porch to talk to Mick.

"That's the first time he's cried since Molly died, at least that I know of. That voyage was like a nightmare. It's not your fault, Mick, but it's amazing that any of us are here to tell about it. This has been a dreadful week for Tommy. I think seeing you just stirred him up. We put little Maureen into the girls' orphanage, so she wouldn't end up in this mill life. Don't get me wrong. It's a far cry from being hungry and I'm grateful for it all; the work, this house and our food. It's just that I can't see anywhere to go from here. We get paid in scrip, only good in the company store and everything is by the grace of that factory over there. I was hoping we could start here and raise up, but I think we might be stuck here forever."

"Hey, but we ain't stuck somewhere starving no more. Maybe we want too much. I can see the rails is gonna' be the same. Not much chance for movin' up. Bad-talking me 'cause I'm Irish. It's better. Maybe that's it. We need to settle for better and not hold out for best."

"I dunno, we've got to have dreams. If we're settling for whatever, we might forget about them. Stop striving for them. But, maybe you're right and it's useless to shoot for best."

"Will you talk to Tommy and tell him not to hate me?"

"Mick, he doesn't hate you. He hates that his mother is dead."

"Right." Mick shrugged. "I suppose I ought to be

getting back across the river soon."

''Yeah, but you don't have to be a stranger. If you get back this way, stop by again. We take Maureen out for picnics some Sundays."

"She might hate me too."

"Nah, I think she was too little to make that connection. So what? You were involved in something that wasn't so good. When you recognized it, you left it. If you'd stayed in it, then you'd be a louse. God knows who the real sinners are. It's always good to see you, Mick"

"You too, Love," Mick hesitated. He started to extend both arms as if to hug, but pulled one back as he saw Erin Marie only extend her hand. One kiss on the cheek later, he turned and walked back down the road as Erin went back in the house to check on Tommy. She wondered if she fell in love with John, would she be striving for best? And if she clung to Mick might she just be settling?

Chapter 22

Off the Block

Charleston, 1852

Slave sale broadsides posted at the entrance to the Charleston market read like a roster. Doctor Newton stood in the morning shade studying the offerings. "Violet, age sixteen, housework and nursemaid: four hundred dollars. Abel, age forty, a rice hand with poor eyesight: five hundred dollars. Happy, age sixty, blacksmith: six hundred dollars. Infant, age one year, likely to be a strong boy: three hundred dollars. Grandison, age thirty-six, strong man: seven hundred dollars."

Newton set down the sack holding his trip provisions and the money chest to scribble a note on a scrap of paper. He skimmed over the remaining ten names and read at the bottom of the poster, "Slaves will be sold separate, or in lots, as best suits the purchaser. Sale will be held rain or shine."

As he entered the courtyard area, he heard wailing. "Please sirs, oh, please, don't take my baby. Just 'cause my masser's dead and gone, don't mean you's have to break up our family."

"Hey, you, come over here." A pudgy white man dragging a whip behind him, walked up to the woman. "I don't want to have to call on my assistant here." He gave the whip a shake. "We can't have no kind of complaining going on here. Now you go on over there, quit that whining and wait your turn."

The woman relented and backed over to a corner, sobbing as her son was led away by his new master.

George Newton took his jacket off and methodically rolled his shirtsleeves, as if he was preparing to birth a baby. The thick humid summer air was heating up. He walked over to the man with the whip, the slave seller.

"Excuse me, sir. May I have a word?"

"Why yes . . . of course." The slave seller noted Newton's well-dressed manner.

"I was wondering of the trust-worthiness of these slaves. I'm from Augusta and, well, we can't risk buying one and having him run off. Seeing that woman separated from her baby made me wonder. Can you tell me something of this strong man?"

"He's coming up next. He'll be a good man. They don't have the same feelings as us white folks. He'll do your bidding if'in you treat him right." The slave seller shook his whip again. "Do you catch my meaning?"

Newton stiffened at the man's suggestion. He stepped back and took his place among the bidders.

The strong man named Grandison was led to the three-foot high square wooden block. A shackle rubbed around his left ankle, and the attached chain was placed over a peg bolt to the left of center. Pearls of perspiration beaded on his massive forehead and then coalesced to form rivulets cascading down to his eyebrows. His sweat either drooled around past his temples or hopped off at the brow and dove directly to the floor. Disproportionately large ears protruded, listening for any hint of his fate. Tightly curled hair, cropped close, framed a face with dark eyes like two muddy pools. A nose of familial likeness traced his tribal ancestry from the West African coast to the South Carolina Gullah Island. Thick parched lips, slightly parted, revealed brightly enameled teeth in vivid contrast to his chocolate-colored skin. A thick trunk of a neck connected head to shoulders. He stood more than six feet tall scraping the hot, mid-morning August sky. A shirtless torso revealed sinewy biceps and abdominal muscles that rippled up beneath his taut skin. His body continued its melting ooze from the sun's continuous overhead beat like a ceremonial drum. From under his loincloth, bulging thighs merged into elongated calves and his broad-based feet were planted as firmly as a tree.

Standing still and silent, Grandison Harris could feel the scrutiny of his potential buyers eyeing him up and down as he squinted into the courtyard.

Someone gestured from the back of the enclosure. Grandison couldn't see who it was. All he could make out were four shadowy hands exchanging something. As he was approached, his foot shackle was lifted from its peg and he was led down the steps from the platform.

He was brought face to face with Doctor Newton who said, "Boy, we'll need to make our preparations. We must move quickly in order to catch the half-past-eleven train." Another pair of hands gave Harris clothes for his journey.

They hurriedly walked the two blocks to the railroad station to catch the steam-powered passenger non-stop that traveled from Charleston to the quaint town of Hamburg, situated across the river from Augusta. On its completion in 1833, the one hundred and thirty six miles of track was touted to be the world's longest railway line and the first to carry the United States mail.

Only after their tickets were purchased and they were seated did the physician begin to explain the intended new life for the slave. "My faculty members and I propose that you will be working for us, that is for me and six other physicians at the Medical College of Georgia. You will have the title of porter, and we will have some specific tasks for you to perform. We want you to be comfortable, to learn to read and write, to advance yourself and in return, we will need to ensure your loyalty. New clothing will be bought for you and we will teach you all about the human body. You're not afraid of evil spirits are you? Do you understand what I'm saying?"

Grandison hadn't uttered a word, yet. Even though this man seemed soft-spoken and kind, he was being taken away from his wife and son on a trek to some foreign place. He wasn't sure he could trust what he was hearing and he was hungry.

Withholding any reply, the future porter closed his eyes as the sunlight moving rhythmically through the trees made kaleidoscopic imprints against his eyes. He leaned back against the seat in the train car. So much was happening so fast. He began to doze, looking for assurance in a dream, but the smell of food jolted him and his grumbling stomach some few minutes later.

"Are you hungry, boy?"

Harris wondered if this man of medicine could read his mind.

Doctor Newton was pulling provisions out of the seemingly bottomless sack he'd brought. He had a loaf of bread, a salted ham slice, some goat cheese and several apples and tomatoes. Both men ravenously ate their fill.

When he was sated, he felt more secure. He turned to Newton and said, "Yez, Mass'r, I sees. This is some good food."

Quickly sitting straight up as if to make a point, the physician responded briskly, "Don't call me that." Surprised by his own inflection, he repositioned his body to match a softer, calmer, tone he continued. "Call me Doctor Newton . . . please. And you are called Grandison?"

Newton's blurted insistence made the slave wary, but the doctor did have kind eyes. He replied, "Yez sir, Grandison Harris, sir."

"Well, Grandison Harris, may we have a long and prosperous association."

"Yez, sir."

They rested back in their seats as the train rolled to the west. After a time, Newton began to fill the noticeable silence, "Have you ever ridden in a train before?"

"No, sir, dis is the first time."

"It won't be your last. We'll see that you get back to Charleston to see your wife and son. That was a nasty business back at the market, a mother being sold separately from her baby. It is not our intention to break up your family."

"I'd be grateful for dat, sir. We sure is movin' fast."

"Good! Do you like it? Would you like for me to tell you about trains? You see, I'm a bit of a railroad enthusiast."

"Yez, sir."

"The Best Friend of Charleston was the name given to the steam engine that first used these tracks. Christmas day, in eighteen-thirty, she debuted. That black puffing locomotive carried one hundred and forty-one people on a six-mile maiden trip. Her passengers thought they were flying on the wings of the wind at a top speed of twenty-five miles an hour."

"It went so fast they didn't have no time to get scared?"

"Right you are. It began a new era in transporting

people and goods. Instead of relying on waterways to be navigable or roads to be passable, the rails could operate in almost any weather. It became so popular, another engine was bought and put into service." Newton paused. "Then, six months later, tragedy struck. Well, it was more like stupidity. A workman tied down a safety valve on the boiler of the Best Friend. He thought the steam was hissing too loudly. Unfortunately, that created a lot of pressure and there was an explosion. It killed him, scalded the engineer and destroyed the engine. So there is a moral to the story. One I want you to heed. That is, if you are not sure of what you are to do, ask questions. We will never reprimand you for asking questions."

"Yez, sir."

"Parts that could be salvaged from the wreckage were used to build another engine named the Phoenix, as it rose from the ashes. The railroad tracks continued to be laid until it was all the way to Hamburg."

Newton pulled his watch by its gold chain from his vest pocket.

"Speaking of Hamburg, we'll be there in less than an hour. We'll have to get off the train and take a horse and buggy across the bridge. There is no railroad connection across the river to Augusta yet. I understand the plans have been laid and construction is to begin, but there certainly was controversy. Hamburg urged building the bridge as a way to connect the western trade all the way from Marthasville to Charleston. The merchants of Augusta have been opposed. I think they're afraid that if trade moves too swiftly though the city it will become merely a way station for the coastal cities. Augusta is in dire need of trade, so they adopted an obstructionist policy toward building a railroad bridge. Boatmen crossing the river have been content with the status quo. The arguments went on for years. Finally now, since

Charleston has threatened to build a railroad line through Rabun Gap and exclude Augusta entirely from the western trade, the city has been forced to change its position. The plan is for the South Carolina Railroad to join rails with the Georgia Railroad next year sometime. Won't that be a wonderful day?"

Newton looked over at Harris, who had fallen fast asleep.

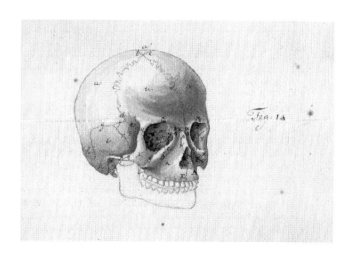

Chapter 23

A Surprise for the Porter

Augusta, 1854

Grandison dragged himself out of bed, still feeling the effects of scaring off the evil spirit. He'd dug up a lot of bodies, but he'd never had a night like last night. He felt confused, but he was already late preparing bodies for the dissection room, so there was no time to ponder the puzzling events. Three cadavers were needed for the tables today. He washed quickly, dressed and set off for the special keeping room.

The whiskey vat, reinforced with metal lining at the corners to prevent leaking, had a middle separator dividing the genders. It could hold up to twelve bodies; six men and six women.

After positioning his stretcher beside the edge, Grandison, with his long grappling hook in hand, walked up the two steps he had built to facilitate his maneuvers.

At that height, even with the top of the vat, he could stretch out and commandeer the bobbing, buoyant bodies over to the side of the vat, reach underneath with both hands and pull them across onto the rolling cot. The steps were more slippery than usual and he lost his footing as he walked up. It was as if some of the contents had spilled out, but he couldn't understand how that could have happened. Steadying himself, he used the hook like a staff to keep from falling.

Once he regained his balance, the porter reached out to place the long grappler around the left arm of the first cadaver. He skillfully maneuvered the male body gently and pulled it over to the side. As soon as the big black man's hulk came up out of the whiskey vat, Harris gasped, "You again? How did you get in there when I takes you back to the cemetery and puts you back in the ground? You must be possessed by some powerful evil spirits. And looks like you gots back to your full heavy weight. Let's see how long your evilness will stay with you whilst you keeps soaking in this whiskey vat. We's got enough other bodies, you is staying here." He lowered the cadaver back into the alcoholic bath and shoved it to float slowly to the opposite side of the vat, close to where the foot was sticking up out of the preservative.

Harris methodically repeated his efforts, lifting out two other males and one female body, setting them on stretchers and continuing his preparations for class. Everything about his routine felt disrupted. Lagging in his chore of rinsing and drying the bodies to reduce the alcohol smell, he pushed each stretcher into the laboratory. He was patting the last male's face when Doctor Campbell came in to prepare for his anatomy sessions.

Henry Campbell pulled his watch by its black braided fob from his right suit vest pocket. "Grandison, I see you are running late with set-ups this morning. Is everything alright?"

"Yez, sir."

"I know we've discussed the importance of caution and secrecy surrounding your work in the past. Are there any problems that I need to know about at the cemetery or with procuring any subjects?"

"There is no evil spirits, right Doctor Campbell?"

Students were beginning to enter the anatomy lab.

"There are no evil spirits, Grandison. Mind your English. We may discuss this in more detail later, if necessary."

"Yez, sir."

Anatomy lab was a time to learn about the human body, to take it apart, examine every inch, look at muscles, bones, corpuscles, veins, arteries, hearts, livers, lungs, kidneys, pancreas, fingers and toes. It was also an opportunity to explore cause of death.

Sterling was assigned at table number two. He pulled on the shoulders of his male subject to reposition and straighten him on the stretcher. The cadaver's head lifted up momentarily and as it fell back, a loud sucking noise came from his mouth. Sterling jumped back from the table and gasped, "What was that?"

Curious students huddled around Sterling and his corpse. Owen brushed by and quipped, "Thank goodness it's not you know who." He checked to make sure no one else heard his comment.

Doctor Campbell sauntered over and began to explain, "Air is ever present in the stomach. Sometimes when pressures change, it will rush out and make noise. It was merely escaping air that made the sucking sound."

Owen whispered to Sterling, "Better mind when you roll him over, the wind might blow the other way as well."

The class dispersed back to their own assigned tables. Noticeably absent was John.

Doctor Campbell remarked, "Does anyone know where Mr. Wilkinson might be this morning?"

Sterling hesitantly spoke up, "I hear he is feeling poorly today, sir."

"Well, unless he's at death's door, I expect there could be no better place to be sick than in a classroom full of medical students."

Most of the classmates laughed at Doctor Campbell's joke, but Sterling found the death reference all too feasible given the nature of John's disappearance. He tried to ward off those thoughts of doom. There had to be some explanation for his disappearance, though, and with each passing hour, he feared with more certainty that he might never see John alive again.

Owen gave Sterling a curious glance in response to his made-up excuse for John.

Grandison Harris not only prepared for all the anatomy and dissecting classes, he attended them as well. He occasionally assisted the students as he continued to learn himself. When Henry Campbell made his quip, Harris studied Sterling's face, but he saw no reaction and his gaze was averted. He pondered John's absence from class and the big black man's reappearing body in the whiskey vat downstairs. He was beginning to feel they must be connected somehow, but his head felt fuzzy. The thread was not apparent. He needed more time to think.

After autopsies were complete, each table gave conference to the entire group on their findings. The students named their subjects for the purpose of discussion.

Table one held Miss P's cadaver. Owen was nominated as his table's spokesman. "This thin young black woman, we judge to be about eighteen years of age. She died from *Negro Consumption*. The official name for the disease is *Struma Africana,* and is considered to be a type of tuberculosis. This condition strikes the young most severely, men and women of color, specifically. We also conclude that based on her physical appearance, she suffered from a nutritional deficiency of vitamin D along with lactose intolerance. Her bones appear much older than the rest of her body indicates."

It was Sterling's turn to speak for table two's specimen. "Our subject, Mr. J, has the appearance of a fifty-year-old Negro male. He has experienced protracted weight loss as evidenced by the loose skin noted on arms, legs and torso. We have reached a consensus that he succumbed to intestinal worms, based on the discovery of their presence in his intestinal tract. We know that worms are endemic here in the South, especially in areas of poor sanitation and hygiene."

Doctor Campbell interjected, "And of course you all have read the article my brother, Robert Campbell, wrote in the eighteen-fifty-one issue of the *Southern Medical and Surgical Journal*, The Morbific Influence of Intestinal Worms. Haven't you?"

Campbell peered out into the group and saw no acknowledgment. "A show of hands, please?"

Meek stares from his students met his gaze.

"Get thee to the library. That article was my brother's attempt to raise awareness to the extent of the condition. I would ask that you all raise your awareness or else!"

A unison "Yes, Sir" was heard from the group.

"All right, then, on to the next."

Purplish colored bruising in a one-inch thick line encircled the neck of Mr. L, a Caucasian male in his forties. The students at table three reported his cause of death as asphyxiation by strangulation. Doctor Campbell concurred and added the subject was a convicted murderer ordered to hang by the neck until dead. "Let me also point out that dissection of an executed criminal is legal in this state. As physicians, we must have a certain awareness of the law. Since that is the case, we were encouraged to collect this subject from the prison two days ago."

Sterling fidgeted as he remembered he was scheduled for dispensary duty from four until six o'clock. He was tired and hungry from his previous night's excursion. Dissections took a long time; it was almost half past three. He brushed by Owen, "I'm slipping out now . . . clinic later. Cover for me, will you?"

"So, John is sick?"

"I felt I had to say something."

Leaving the rest of the cleanup to his classmates, Sterling stealthily and without notice headed out toward Mrs. Gardner's boarding house. His thoughts turned to Gracie, the cook, and how she could so quickly warm up a plate of food. He wondered if John, wherever he was, had an appetite.

Gracie didn't disappoint Sterling. She set a steaming plate of collard greens, mashed potatoes, pulled pork and cornbread in front of him.

"Where is Mrs. Gardner? I didn't see her when I came in and I thought she'd be spinning away. Didn't Owen fix her wheel?"

Gracie became sullen, and looked away. "I don't knows what is going on around here anymore. And I's not saying nothing about nothing."

"Whatever do you mean, Gracie?"

Chapter 24

Addiction

Amanda woke up without her memory. She had a splitting headache as well. Vaguely remembering Owen helping with her spinning wheel, the remainder of the evening's events seemed to float somewhere between consciousness and a dream memory. She knew she had wanted to kiss him and she thought she remembered his lips touching hers; soft, wet, groping tongues. But she wasn't sure. Did they dance to their own music? She thought she remembered lying down in the best room bed, but now she found herself in her own bedroom on the second floor. Feeling under the covers, she found herself undressed and in her nightgown, but she had no memory of disrobing and certainly no recollection of release from her whalebone corset.

Dizziness overcame her as she stood up and, trying to secure her footing, she leaned against the wall. Moving to the dry sink basin, she splashed cool water from the pitcher onto her face. *Gracie has been up here with fresh water already this morning*, she thought. Donning her favorite blue dressing gown, waves of nausea came over her. *Perhaps tea will help*. She pulled the bell cord to ring for Gracie. After waiting a few minutes with no response, she impatiently began to make her way to the landing. "Why must I do so much for myself all the time?" She was grumpily muttering to no one.

Holding tightly to the banister, she started down the stairs.

Gracie came around the corner and met Amanda mid-flight. She grabbed onto her elbow to assist. "I just don't know what is wrong with me this morning."

"It isn't morning anymore, Miss Amanda. It's late in the afternoon. Mister Sterling is back from his studies already and eating his dinner. I sees Mister Owen this morning for breakfast, but I hasn't caught sight of Mister John at all today. He didn't so much as mess his bed covers last night."

"Perhaps I'm sick, if I slept the whole day."

Amanda tiptoed into the dining room trying not to further upset her head, "Sterling, do you have any idea what is going on around here?"

"I'm not sure to what you are referring, Mrs. Gardner."

"I think you know quite well to what I refer. Gracie here tells me that your compatriot, John, hasn't put the slightest rumple into his bed covers last night and neither hide nor hair has been seen of him. Do you have knowledge of what has happened to him?" She slumped into the armchair at the head of the table. "Gracie, some tea please."

"You needs something else to eat, ma'am."

"No, Gracie, just the tea. I feel awful."

Turning her attention back to Sterling, "Would you please tell me?"

Sterling studied his landlady's face. He thought she looked extraordinarily pale with dark circles under her brown eyes. The tidy bun she had sported the previous night now had thick strands of her brunette hair hanging in disarray.

"Mrs. Gardner, I can't speak to John's whereabouts," was Sterling's only response. In his attempt to display no emotion, he felt his face flush as he hurried to finish his dinner. He began to wonder if his answer had been too curt and hasty. In order to dispel any suspicion and delay further discussion he added, "I think he might be doing some special project with one of the doctors over at the hospital."

She shot him a curious glance. "I wonder what sort of project that might be?"

"I'm not certain, but it seems to be shrouded in secrecy." Sterling thought better of continuing with his confabulation. He changed the subject. "Please thank Gracie ever so much for a scrumptious dinner, Mrs. Gardner." Along with his statement he nearly flew out the door to begin his walk over to the Jackson Street Hospital dispensary.

As Sterling turned onto Broad, he spied Miss Lucy Clark on the other side of the street. She looked beautiful, dressed in modest black. The color contrasted starkly with her peachy complexion and strawberry blonde hair. Although he looked tired and disheveled, he was feeling bold, pleased with himself for squirming around Mrs. Gardner's questions about John. Besides, he was smitten and didn't want to miss an opportunity to say hello.

He apologized in advance, "Dear Miss Lucy, please forgive my appearance. I fear I must look dreadful, but my self-consciousness does little to restrain me from saying 'hello'. I so wanted to see you."

"Why, Sterling Adams, what a nice happenstance.

Medical school must be extraordinarily difficult. What else could you look but dreadful, what with staying up so late every night to study?" Lucy glanced at him playfully and maintained her poise, but her body swayed slightly in an inviting sort of way. "I rest assured that you are a good student, because you've dedicated yourself so."

Sterling's fair skin blushed. "Oh, Miss Lucy, you flatter me with such praise. Thank you. I hope to be seeing you again. Actually, I would be honored to know that I might be received to come calling on you one day soon."

"That would be lovely," she smiled sweetly at him.

"Good day then." With that, Sterling crossed the street toward the infirmary. Whistling a happy melody, he wondered what she would really think of him if she knew about John's prank or what he'd done with a dead body. She was so unsuspecting. And his naïveté was certainly diminishing quickly.

Owen had finished with the cleanup and was on his way to the boarding house for his dinner as he passed by Sterling in front of the hospital. "Did you get something to eat?"

"Yes, thanks for looking out for me. There's something else going on at the house. You'd better take care of Mrs. Gardner, she looks perfectly awful today."

"In what way?"

"I'm not sure what's ailing her but she looks tired, pale and downright sickly. And she's asking questions about John."

"Yes, well I have questions about John, myself."

"I've got to hurry, can't be late for clinic." Sterling evasively darted though the front door of the hospital.

Owen hurried back to Mrs. Gardner's and met a cool reception first from Broom who was out back chopping wood and then from Gracie who was washing Sterling's dishes.

"Go sit down in the dining room with Miss Amanda and I'll get your dinner ready."

"Is something wrong?"

"I ain't saying nothing about nothing."

Owen thought the servants were acting peculiar. He entered the dining room and looked at Amanda. She did appear sickly. It was as though her skin had turned milky pale and her eyes belonged to raccoons with their dark circles. They exchanged awkward glances.

"What happened last night, Owen?"

"I was about to ask you the very same question."

"Well?"

"Nothing, as far as I know."

"Have you ruined my reputation?" Amanda voice was getting louder.

"Your reputation? What are you talking about?"

"I have no memory of last night."

"We worked on your spinning wheel . . . I oiled it and we determined that it was running smoothly once again. Then I guess you could say that we had a little merriment."

"A little merriment? Did we kiss?"

Owen blushed, "We did kiss."

"And then what?"

"Then, nothing."

"Really? Nothing?"

"Correct. We kissed a few times and we sort of danced into the best room, but you passed out."

"I passed out?"

"Yes, I couldn't understand it. We only had two swigs of whiskey in our tea and you passed out. I'd think even a genteel woman like you could hold her liquor better than that." Owen's attempt at lightheartedness rang more of condescension.

"What makes you think I'm so genteel?" Amanda

sneered.

Their conversation clamped into silence as Gracie interrupted when she set a plate of food before Owen and a pot of tea at Amanda's place. Sensing the tension, she left the room without speaking.

Owen studied Amanda, musing curiously how he could have been so attracted to her the night before. He wondered if she had ever seduced other students, other boarders. Had he been swayed off course by her, or had male desire simply overcome him? Feeling pity and disrespect at the same time, but also relief that there had been no real union, he sat quietly, hoping there would be no scene.

"Didn't we do anything?"

"No, Mrs. Gardner, as I've already explained, you passed out. I put a pillow under your head."

"How did I end up in my own bedroom?"

"I have no idea. You were in the best room bed when I put the pillow under your head and then . . . I'm not certain, because I fell asleep as well. The next thing I remember is waking up to Sterling's heavy steps on the staircase. I got up to see what was happening. He needed my assistance with a sick patient down at the tavern."

"Oh, no. Did he see us together in the best room bed?"

"No, he had no idea about that. I met him up on the stair landing."

"I thought you cared about me."

"I do care about you. I certainly care about your health and I'm quite curious about why you were so overcome with the whiskey last night. Do you take other medicines?"

"Always the medical student, eh? Yes, I take this three times a day."

Amanda reached into her dressing gown pocket and pulled out a small brown bottle of liquid with a stopper top. "Ten drops in my tea" and she proceeded to drip them by into her cup while she counted.

"And what is it for?"

"It's laudanum, you fool." Amanda had developed an edge in her voice. "It helps me with my female sensibilities and it makes the world less sharp, less painful. It was prescribed for me when Paul died and I've taken it ever since. The chemist mixes my dosage and provides me with a regular supply."

"That explains why you passed out. The alcohol you drank potentiated the effects of the laudanum. It was as though you took two or three times your normal dose. And that also explains why you are feeling so poorly today."

"Explaining it doesn't give my memory back to me." Her tone softened, Amanda began to sob. She felt humiliated and ashamed at not remembering how she got into her own bed. She still wasn't completely convinced that she hadn't been taken advantage of, but she had to admit that Owen did have a gentle manner. He was probably telling the truth. "Oh, I'm so confused about what all is going on."

Owen had finished eating his dinner and pushed the plate to the side. He stood up and lightly caressed Amanda's shoulders.

"There, there, Mrs. Gardner."

"Wouldn't you consider calling me Amanda, especially after last night?"

Owen removed his hands and sat back down. "Really, we were simply having a little fun. At least that is what I perceived. I apologize if you thought it was more."

Amanda dried her eyes with her napkin and turned her attention to the missing student. "Do you know where John is?"

"No, I don't."

"Sterling said something about him working on a special project. What sort of secret research project would keep him out all night? I worry about all of my young men when things don't seem right, but particularly if someone doesn't make it home at night. Perhaps he's had an accident. Maybe I should go and talk with Doctor Campbell."

"A special project with the medical school? I hadn't heard of anything, but I suppose there could be something. I wouldn't talk to Doctor Campbell if I were you."

"And why not?"

Surely he and Sterling would become involved in an investigation of some sort if Amanda insisted on talking with Doctor Campbell. Inquiries might happen anyway if John didn't make an appearance soon, but he hoped to forestall them as long as possible. He had to convince Amanda that it was not a good idea. He thought quickly and said, "Doctor Campbell was in quite a state today in class. He seemed angry. It might only make matters worse to stir him. I'll admit that John does seem to be missing at the moment. He mentioned a certain young lady he's become smitten with and he talked about asking her to our holiday social, but I don't even know her name, let alone where she lives. He wasn't in attendance in our anatomy class, that's true, but as to where he's gone, it's a mystery. Perhaps he is sick somewhere or he might have had an accident, or maybe he is working on some special project or maybe he just got lost in the young woman's fancy. We should be patient and see what happens." In an attempt to divert her attention he asked, "Is your spinning wheel still working smoothly?"

"I've got such a throbbing head, I haven't even checked. But you said we did fix it last night?"

"It was working perfectly last night."

"I was hoping other things would work perfectly last night." Amanda leaned across the table and touched Owen's arm. "Don't you care about me, Owen? I thought we might have something together. I'm so ashamed of my thoughts. I may as well just drown them."

He pulled away gently, "Amanda, please don't talk that way. Let's see how things look when you are recovered from your spree of overindulgence. It's not really your fault. I would never have offered you the whiskey if I'd known you were taking laudanum. I wager that by tomorrow you will be feeling better about everything." He rose from the table. "A little smile before I go?" He lifted her chin slightly. "I must run off to the library and read several articles and then stop in at the hospital to visit a patient."

Amanda forced a half smile

Owen turned and gathered his coat, hat and gloves and left through the front door. He was quite relieved to be leaving the emotionally stormy house. Like a raging sea, Amanda's waves were insistent. He was uncomfortable at her suggestions of romantic entanglement, her urgent demand for his care. He was having a playful romp with her and he thought she was like-minded. She was older than any woman he'd ever envisioned in his fantasies. He hoped John's return would calm the waters and they could get back to the way things used to be. Presently, any excuse for getting away and staying away would do.

Amanda slumped in her chair, her mood turning maudlin. *I usually take ten drops in my tea, but today I will take ten times ten. Paul left me to the wind. I have no reason to live. No children, no hope for romance, nothing. I can't even seduce a young man. My looks are leaving me and I fear my figure too. I'll put myself out of this misery of life once and for all.*

Pouring the remainder of the ruby-colored concoction

of opium, honey, licorice, camphor, anise and wine into her cup of tea, she resolutely lifted it to her lips.

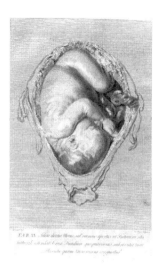

TAB. XX. *Idea chorae Uteri, ad mentem affectus ut Foetus in Naturali situ iacet ubi Cava Cordeus praegnantiae adest ubi homo laeviter quum Deus excurvi applicat.*

Chapter 25

Monsters

On October 19, 1854 at three o'clock in the afternoon, Doctor Joseph Adams Eve was called out to assist with a delivery. Mrs. S, a twenty-one year old had been taken into labor eleven hours previously. She was attended by a midwife, but as her labor was not progressing, the physician was summoned.

Doctor Eve was a kind man and so thoughtful of others it is said that he saluted lampposts and trees on his big pony, fearing he might miss greeting a pedestrian. He was peculiarly courteous and loving.

Miss Wilson, the midwife, was anxiously awaiting Doctor Eve's arrival. She heard his carriage and was standing at the open door.

"Oh, Doctor Eve, I've never seen anything like this in all my days of attending to the birthing of babies. I'm so glad you've arrived." She wrung her hands as she continued. "I've tried everything I know to do, and nothing is working. Thank goodness you're here."

During his medical schooling, Joseph Eve studied with a professor who told him, as if it were a pearl of wisdom, "As long as a nurse is obedient, the more ignorant she is, the better. A smart nurse will only question a physician's judgment. The nurse should have only sense enough to obey orders. Dumb nurses would be ideal in all critical cases."

Doctor Eve did not share his instructor's sentiments, as he never found it to be true about the nurses or midwives he'd worked with. He had assisted Miss Wilson on several other occasions and knew her to be a capable and level-headed practitioner.

"Doctor Eve, the head of this child delivered almost four hours ago. Mrs. S has continued to have violent pains, but they are ineffectual. The baby was at first alive, I am quite certain. I inserted a finger into its mouth and the lips moved."

"Miss Wilson, please go and request a servant to brew us a pot of tea."

Doctor Eve moved to the side of the bed where Mrs. S lay. He placed his hand on hers in a reassuring manner. She turned toward him, her eyes wracked with pain and concern.

"Doctor, something must be terribly wrong with my baby."

"I'm not sure why you are so distressed in your labor. But I'm here to find out. Please relax as much as you can, while I examine the situation."

Miss Wilson came back into the room. "Tea will be here shortly, sir."

Doctor Eve knelt on the bed between Mrs. S's legs as he spread them wide apart and found the head of her child trapped and inert; its neck not yet visible. He proceeded with great difficulty to bring down one arm and shoulder and then the other. Delivery was still not progressing as he would have expected. He then encountered an enlargement of the abdomen, some other form of deformity.

"Mrs. S, I will require you to bear down with all your strength when I direct you." Miss Wilson's experienced hands patted Mrs. S's arm and swabbed her perspiring forehead.

He waited for her next uterine contraction and placed as much traction as he felt safe and proper. Mrs. S strained and pushed as two females were finally delivered. They were united by their breasts and abdomen as low down as the umbilicus. Neither one was alive.

"Why isn't my baby crying?"

"Mrs. S, I'm so sorry to tell you that your babies have been born dead. Two daughters."

Mrs. S. whimpered in resigned exhaustion.

The maidservant delivered a pot of tea with three cups and left the room hurriedly.

Doctor Eve instructed Miss Wilson to wrap the babies in a blanket. He hoped that Mrs. S would not insist on laying eyes on them as he intended not to tell her of their conjoined nature.

He delivered her placenta and spoke to her in a calming manner. "Mrs. S, my dear woman, you have been laboring for quite some time and I am certain that this result comes as a supreme disappointment to you. However, I hope you will take comfort in the fact that you may have opportunities for other babies. He added ten drops of laudanum to Mrs. S's cup and instructed her to drink it. The solution of opium in alcohol was considered a cure-all. "Miss Wilson will help you with the tea, I am going to speak to your husband. I will be return shortly."

Doctor Eve found Mr. S pacing in the study.

"How is she, Doctor Eve?"

"Your wife is doing well and she will be able to have other children." Eve shook his head. "Unfortunately this pregnancy was doomed. Two twin daughters, but they were delivered in an unlucky manner. Heart trouble, I'd say." He diplomatically skirted around their conjoined nature.

"May I see my wife?"

"Yes, but only briefly. I've given her something for pain and she is exhausted after the struggle she had with delivery. I was wondering if you would consider allowing me to take the twins back to the Medical College as illustrative models. We can learn so much from such examples, if our patients will permit."

"I would have no issue with that, sir. You have graciously given of your time and talent and kept my wife alive. I will speak with her about it, should she ask."

"Thank you, Mr. S. Please come with me."

While Mr. S. sat on the bed comforting his wife, Doctor Eve and Miss Wilson placed the blanket-wrapped twins in a secured compartment in his buggy parked outside. Mrs. S was resting quietly as Doctor Eve instructed Miss Wilson. "Stay with her until tomorrow to monitor for any excessive bleeding. Will you?"

"Yes, sir. I certainly will do that. Thank you, Doctor Eve."

As the physician steered his horse-drawn buggy back to Augusta, he couldn't help but think that it was a blessing, both to the babies and their parents that they had been born dead. He thought it was a sort of kind and merciful dispensation of providence.

Doctor Eve preserved the adherent fetuses in whiskey. Their glass jar display served as a teaching example for his class lecture on abnormal pregnancy.

"One of the most unexplainable laws pertaining to the development of monsters is that of symmetry. However strangely and variously two or more fetuses may be connected, similar parts are always found united. We never observe an arm attached to a leg or leg to hand or side to a back or a back of one to abdomen of another. It is a natural curiosity of nature and her freaks. In this particular instance, death of the first might have been determined by the long continual violent labor, or by tractions made on the head, or it may have been consequent to the death of the second. The amount of force employed in their delivery was by no means excessive. Certainly the death of one must necessarily have involved the death of the other, as there was but one common heart for both. There is little doubt that both were alive when labor commenced."

JACKSON STREET HOSPITAL

AND

SURGICAL INFIRMARY,
FOR NEGROES,
AUGUSTA, GEORGIA.

Chapter 26

The Remedy

Gracie returned to the dining room with the intention of clearing dishes when she found Amanda slumped in the chair, her empty cup knocked over on its side. "Miss Amanda . . . Miss Amanda." She patted her left hand. "What's happened to you?" She noted the empty brown medicine bottle and ran to the back door, swung it open wide and hollered, "Broom come in here, quick. It's Miss Amanda."

"What's wrong?"

"Just look at her, she's done it again. You'd better hitch up the horse so we can take her to see a doctor."

"We won't need the horse. It's only two blocks. I'll carry her. Get me a blanket."

"You're going to carry her to the Jackson Street Infirmary?"

"It's much closer than the City Hospital."

"But, it's for us colored folks."

"Isn't that where Sterling is working today? He'll make sure she gets seen. It'll be all right. Let's hurry."

The Campbell brothers had recently opened a new surgical infirmary for Negroes. Both physicians believed it would provide excellent teaching opportunities for medical students. It was a modern facility with hot and cold running water and fifty beds.

Gracie found a white woolen blanket. Broom wrapped her up like a caterpillar in a cocoon and took off out the back door, running with the stride of his bushman's heritage.

"You go on, I'm following close behind." Gracie was struggling to keep up with his pace.

Sterling was on receiving duty when he intercepted the runner with his load at the front door of the hospital.

"Broom, what in the world are you doing here? Is something wrong with Gracie?"

"No, Mister Sterling, look, it's Miss Amanda." He pulled the blanket from over her head.

"What's happened? Put her over here." Sterling pointed to a stretcher.

Gracie had caught up. "Miss Amanda took this." She handed the empty bottle of laudanum to Sterling. "She did the same thing about three years ago." Henry Campbell came around the corner to join them.

"An overdose? How much did she take?"

"Half a bottle, but I have a confession to make." Gracie huddled up with Sterling and Doctor Campbell. "I watered this bottle down some with red wine this morning. You see, she was acting strange. I woke up in the middle of the night. I don't know what woke me, but I came in the house to check on things. I found her asleep in the downstairs best room with all her clothes on. Knocked out, she was. I can tell when she's getting sad, since she's been like this before. I went and woke Broom and we carried her up to her room, and dressed her for bed. She slept nearly all day. I checked on her several times. When she did wake up, she didn't feel well. I made her some tea and I thought she was doing better. Then I overheard her and Mr. Owen having a spat at dinner. I was wondering if the two of them have been up to something, but I didn't say nothing. When I come back to clear the table, he was gone and I found her knocked out again with this empty bottle next to her."

"But you had diluted it?"

"Yes, sir."

"So, if it was half full and you poured out half and replaced it with red wine, she couldn't have gotten a lethal dose. You might have saved your mistress, Gracie."

"That was what I was hoping for, Doctor."

"I think you folks will be able to take her home shortly."

Sterling began to wheel the stretcher toward a treatment room.

"How would you handle this?" Doctor Campbell quizzed Sterling.

"I'd bleed her until she started to arouse, not more than one hundred cubic centimeters. Then I'd send her home with instructions for several cups of strong black coffee."

"Excellent, I agree with your treatment plan. She won't need to have her stomach purged. You begin. I will check on the patient across the hall and return shortly."

Owen, after finishing his reading at the library and visiting his patient, went looking for Sterling. He was hoping to confide in his friend about Amanda Gardner's disturbing behavior.

He peered into the room where Sterling was bloodletting and was shocked to see that the patient was Amanda.

"Sterling, what is going on?"

"Mrs. Gardner, old chap. Overdose."

"Oh, no. What do you think caused it?"

"I don't know. The servants say that it's happened before."

"Really? When?"

"Gracie said a couple of years ago. Last night she and Broom found her asleep in the best room and they took her up to bed. They said she was knocked out. I'm not sure what to make of it. Remember, I saw her while I was eating dinner and she looked perfectly dreadful then."

"Too much laudanum, perhaps? So Gracie and Broom took her up to her room?"

"Yes, and Gracie mentioned that you'd been acting suspicious, Owen."

"I hope nobody thinks I gave her the stuff."

"I doubt it, since it's happened before. Just lay low."

"Right... see you later. I'm going home now." Owen left out the back door to avoid seeing the servants who were waiting to take Amanda home.

Sterling concluded his treatment on the still groggy landlady as Doctor Campbell returned to the room.

"I was wondering if you would share your thoughts about her continued use of laudanum, Doctor Campbell."

"I think we should notify the chemist to discontinue her supply. What would you recommend in its place?"

"Morphine tablets?"

"Agreed. That is a good choice. Less chance for addiction and perhaps fewer mood swings. You're doing a fine job there, Mr. Adams."

"Thank you, sir."

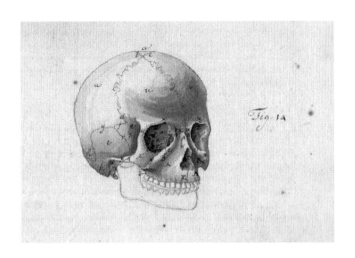

Chapter 27

Awakening

John was having alternating visions of mangled fingers and a beautiful woman. Both were unclear. In the pitch dark his head throbbed as he tried to recall his last memory. *We were going to play a prank on the porter. I remember the Resurrection Man had a body in the back of his wagon. We moved that heavy specimen and I got into the bag smelling of death. The wagon jolted and jostled for a long time. I couldn't get out of the bag. There was a loud whack, then blinding pain and blank. Where in the world could this be, so cramped, dark and cold? I can feel my legs and wiggle my toes. My right arm moves, but the left hurts.*

John performed a physical assessment on himself in his anatomically trained manner.

Curling his right arm in its tight space, he reached up to feel his face and found burlap over his nose and mouth. He stretched to the top of his head, felt for the edge of the bag and brought it down over his face. Some dirt fell into his mouth, but he spit it back out. He pulled the coarse material down past his other arm with small wriggling movements.

Panic was only seconds away and the sense of drowning in a waterless sea of soil made him focused. With his right arm free, he groped above his head, finding more dirt and various sized wooden fragments. He felt for the biggest piece, grabbed it by curving his knuckles around it and pushed, using it like a scraper to plow through the earth. He knew where he was now, gripped with the realization of being buried alive, but fighting it for fear it would paralyze his escape efforts. "No time for that. I must keep pressing. Please let this air pocket stay with me so I can breathe," he uttered his desperate plea while panting with exertion.

There seemed to be a track of soft soil that moved easily as he pushed up and back. John was able to bend his knees slightly and writhe like an earthworm. When his feet had sufficient clearance, he pushed down hard to rip the burlap at the bottom of the bag. As soon as he was past the open part of the coffin where the top had been partially removed, he could push more forcefully with his feet. His arm suddenly found free air with no more dirt. The earth released him. Sucking in a big gasp of fresh night air, the most delicious breath he could ever remember, it was chilly as it bit his lungs.

Hooting through the darkness, an owl raised his voice in Cedar Grove. John was almost completely free of the confined space where he'd spent the last eighteen hours. Two more pushes with his feet. Attempting to stand, his knees buckled. He looked down at his left, limp arm and concluded it was fractured. Relieved that he could see no bone sticking through his skin, he ran his hands over his face. He felt several globs of dried blood above his left temple. Steadying himself again, he stood up and noticed dispersed trinkets and a blanket and he wondered if someone had come to this site to mourn.

Cradling his left arm in his right to keep it still and minimize the pain, he started a slow trek back in the direction of the Medical College. The autumn moon, a full, huge glowing ball of orange, was beginning its rise over the horizon.

• • •

Sterling's shift had lasted longer than usual due to a particularly large demand for cough syrup. After he handed out his last bottle, he hung up his white apron and walked mindlessly out into the evening air toward the direction of Cedar Grove Cemetery. *Maybe if I go there, I'll find some clues about John's whereabouts.*

He'd gone almost two blocks when he saw what looked like a specter before him. Sterling could feel the hair on the back of his neck stand up. "John… is that you?"

"Strawling, I never thought I'd be so happy to see your mug. Help me out here old buddy, will you? I've got to go and see a beautiful young woman and a young lad."

"My goodness, what has happened to you? Where in the world have you been? You're filthy and bleeding and talking crazy… and… well, we'll need to have a better look at you."

John collapsed into his friend's waiting arms.

"Come on, let's go to the infirmary. I just came from there. Doctor Campbell's gone home. I'll patch you up and you can tell me all about it." Sterling placed John's right arm around his neck and hugged him around the waist as the two hobbled back toward Jackson Street.

"Okay, but I've got to go and invite Erin Marie to the holiday social. And Tommy… I've got to see that Tommy goes to medical school. My mind is made up."

"You must have gotten a nasty bump on that head of yours. I'm just so glad to see that you're alive."

"Me, too. As best as I can figure, after I got into the sack and the horse ran away, I guess the porter saw me move and he must have smacked me with a shovel or something. I remember that he said something about an evil spirit, but then my lights went out. I must have lain in the grave for some time, but I faded in and out, so I don't know for how long. I think I heard some moaning and crying going on. But that's about all. When I came to my senses, I managed to push my way out. Hey, what happened to that body we deposited in the alley?"

"Now you're talking. You left me with quite a mess. I got Owen to help me take him to the whiskey room. We put him in the preservative. I think the porter must have flipped when he saw that big one in the vat, because the last time he saw that body, it was in the bag."

"How long was I really gone? Did anyone miss me?"

"You were lost for the better part of a whole twenty-four hours. Doctor Campbell asked where you were. I told him you were feeling poorly. He seemed to buy that. Mrs. Gardner wanted to know where you were last night, but I'm not sure she's in any shape to be asking."

"What do you mean by that?"

"She was a patient of ours tonight. Laudanum overdose."

"Mrs. Gardner? I find that hard to believe. Is she alright?"

"She looked rather awful when I saw her earlier, but Doctor Campbell said she'll be fine. Maybe she tried to kill herself because you didn't come home last night."

"Nonsense! Get serious will you? I've had enough of jokes and pranks. No more for me. I've just been released from the clutches of death and I want to make the most out of this second chance."

"Seeing you become serious is something I'll enjoy watching. And speaking of second chances, apparently it's not the first time Mrs. Gardner has tried to commit suicide."

"Just look what all happens when I go away for a day. Come on Strawling, help me clean up so we can have a look at this arm, will you?"

"Right away, Doctor Serious."

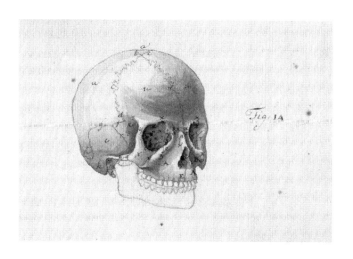

Chapter 28

A Switch

Grandison swept the floor in the special keeping room. Both Doctors Newton and Campbell had assured him that there were no evil spirits to fear, but he wasn't sure he believed them. He sat down on the second step leading up to the whiskey vat and began talking to himself. "If that big black man I digs up is now in this vat, then who is it I puts back in the grave? The only persons I knows of that ain't where he ought to be is Mister John. What if he be the one I done smacked with the shovel? Can't have no white bones in the black cemetery. What if I'd killed a white man? This is terrible trouble."

He buried his face in his hands. He'd been in denial about the possibility. Now dread flooded over him.

He hitched Bessie and went over to Mr. Callahan's to charge a new pine burial box to the Medical College. No questions asked. Grandison often picked up coffins and burial shrouds for folks who'd died at either Jackson

Street or City Hospitals.

After placing the coffin on top of the stretcher, he fished Jacob Brown's body out of its whiskey bath and shoved it up and over the edge of the box. Starting at the feet and pulling up, he covered the body with a burial shroud. "No need to wash and dry you. You're presentable enough. No one is ever going to see you."

Grandison waited until after midnight to begin his trip to Cedar Grove. The moon, now high in the sky, lit his wagon's pathway with its bright shade of white.

"What is I gonna' do with Mister John's dead body if he be the one that's in the grave? I gots to think of something. Sure can't takes him to the anatomy class." He talked to his horse as though he expected her to answer.

Reaching the graveside, Grandison immediately noticed that things were out of order. The burial place had been disturbed. Mementos were strewn, a blanket was rumpled up and there was a gaping hole at the right side of the site with loose dirt all around.

"If somebody else has already been here . . . come and found him . . . and digs him up, I mights be fixin' to be a dead man, too."

Harris carefully moved the blanket and memorabilia under the tree and re-dug the rest of the grave. Removing bits of broken pinewood, he dragged out the remainder of the old coffin and cracked off the rest of the top. There was nothing there except an empty, ripped burlap bag.

"Maybe somebody's playin' tricks on me, follows me down last night, dug this body up after I'd put him in the ground and takes him back to the whiskey vat. No, that don't explain the change in weights. The one I takes from here last night was heavy, but the one I done smacked and put back in here was light and the body in this here coffin is heavy again. I wish I could tells old Doc Newton what's going on . . . but he'd be so mad wit me for thinking about spirits."

Placing the debris into the back of his wagon, Grandison finished cleaning up the old gravesite. He pushed Jacob Brown's new coffin into the hole. "May you rest in peace now. I's so sorry 'bout it all."

He mounded the dirt up high and meticulously positioned the articles around the grave as he imagined they had been placed; the charms, and the blanket laid out smooth, like a patch of grass.

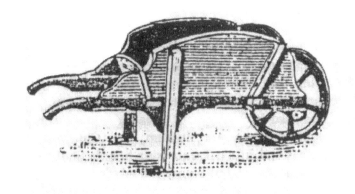

Chapter 29

Moving Day

Mary Brown sat on a stoop surrounded by her possessions as Jacob's brother, Samuel, walked up pushing a wheelbarrow.

"Good morning to you, Mary. Are you ready to get loaded up and move your things?"

"You knows I's grateful to you, Sammy." Jacob's youngest brother could have passed for his identical twin. He'd always been Mary's favorite out of Jacob's six brothers.

"Mary, now you knows it ain't no bother. Since Clara passed and the children have gotten grown . . . it'll be good to have some company. Besides, you'll earn your keep."

Mary helped load the cart.

"I has a strange thing happen yesterday at the cemetery. I's putting out charms to keep Jacob happy in his new resting place an' when I tells him that I gots to move, I thinks I hears him moan. It was a low, soft moan. I barely heard it, so I asks him if he's not at rest to holler up louder so as I could be sure, but I never did hear no more."

"Mary, do you thinks he could be buried alive? You heard tell about how some folks puts a bell on the end of a stick?"

She shook her head no.

"That there stick goes into the coffin, resting against the chest of the dead person. That way if some folks ain't all dead . . . I means if they comes back to life after they's been put in the ground. When they breathes, the bell rings and folks'll knows to dig 'em back up."

"Samuel, has you been drinking this early in the day?"

"No, sure enough. There's a kind of condition that makes folks look dead, but they's not."

"Shut your mouth!"

"I's meaning it Mary. Maybe we needs to go see about Jacob. And you knows what else? Some folks 'round here wonders if there's any grave robbing going on. We might find out about that, too."

"Grave robbing? No, Samuel."

The in-law siblings stepped up their pace and after depositing Mary's belongings at Samuel's house, walked over to Cedar Grove Cemetery.

On the opposite side of Watkins Street, Grandison Harris stood aghast. He had been pacing through the neighborhood trying to shake off the cloud of doom he felt hovering over him from not knowing what had happened to John. Now, looking at the man with Mary, he was sure he was looking at a walking dead man. He muttered to himself, "But it can't be, there must be some other 'xplanation," as he hurried back to the anatomy lab to prepare his set-up work.

Samuel and Mary were engaged in conversation and

took no notice of him as they turned into the cemetery's arched entrance.

Seeing Jacob's gravesite, Mary swooned and grabbed her relative's arm. "Samuel, that mound looks bigger than yesterday. You don't suppose it's from Jacob's breath? And the charms is all misplaced. You think he's turning over in there trying to gets out?"

"I dunno, Mary. Maybe we needs to get a shovel and dig him up to see for sure."

Walking over to the cemetery office, Samuel found no caretaker, but he did find a shovel. Mary removed her mementos.

Samuel made quick work of digging in the soft earth. He jumped down in the hole, uncovering the full length of the casket and heaving dirt to the opposite side from where Mary was peering. As Samuel lifted the top off of the box, they both reeled from the strong odor of alcohol.

Mary spoke to him, "Jacob Brown, what was you drinking when you gots dead?"

She dropped to her knees, covered her eyes with both hands and sobbed.

Samuel turned the top of the coffin in Mary's direction. "Look, there's no clawed scratches on the top."

"I can't looks no more. I's all done in."

"Well, he's been dead alright. Must've been that active 'magination of yours that heard that moaning. Pay your last respects again and I covers him back up."

Still sobbing, but with a tone of sarcasm in her voice Mary said, "My 'magination? You's the one that said he might have needed a bell."

Chapter 30

Mill House Meeting

John remembered exactly where the McLennans lived. The shotgun mill house was drab and like all the others on the outside, but inside it had a warm, inviting, homey feel. It had been almost two years since Tommy's accident. John couldn't wait to see them.

Rapping noisily on the door, he wondered how he'd be received. Tommy flung it open as he squealed, "Auntie, look who's here. It's Mister Doctor John."

"Invite him in, Tommy. Don't keep him standing out in the cold."

Erin Marie came from the kitchen wiping her hands on a bright green apron covering her clothes. The color of an emerald, it offset her flaming hair. She looked even more beautiful than John had remembered.

"We haven't seen you in a long while, Mister Doctor John." Erin looked over at Tommy's admiring stare.

Tommy held his hand up for inspection. "I can make

these three fingers work real good now." He was gently patting John's white sling. "What happened to your arm?"

"Tommy boy, I fell into a big hole and had trouble getting out. I broke my arm and Erin . . . you are quite correct, it has been way too long since I've seen the two of you. Will you both please call me John?"

"Would you like a cup of tea, John? We were about to have our evening cup."

"That would be splendid. Thank you."

"Why don't you two sit at the table and I'll prepare it."

"What else is on your arm besides that white cloth holding it up?" Tommy's curious nature led him to peer all around and inside John's hanging bandage.

"This outer wrap is called a sling and inside is a splint. See, there is a straight piece of stiff board and my arm is wrapped to it. That will keep it still and in place until the bone knits itself back together."

"Bones knit? I thought that was something Auntie did to make a sweater."

John chuckled, "We say bones knit together. It means they're mending . . . healing. Have you started with your reading lessons?"

"Yes, sir. I've finished with the first primer already."

"That is wonderful news. May I start bringing you journal articles to read soon?"

"I'm not sure about that. What is a journal article?"

"It's like a magazine for doctors. The *Southern Medical and Surgical Journal* is the one I read mostly. There are many things to learn, and new advances of which to be aware. There is a lot of work to being a doctor. Are you still resolved?"

"It's the only thing he talks about." Erin brought in the tea and freshly baked Irish soda bread.

"Hmm . . . this smells good. What is it?"

"It's our version of a kind of sweet bread made with buttermilk. There are raisins in it."

"It's really good, John." Tommy mumbled with a mouthful.

"Let's see, Tommy .   mmm, quite tasty. You are certainly right about that!"

"You can even dunk the ends in your tea. That's good, too." Tommy gave a demonstration of his technique.

"Erin Marie, I was wondering if you'd be available to accompany me to the Medical College's holiday social in four weeks' time?" John blurted out his question as if he could not keep it to himself a second longer.

She looked slightly stunned, but recovered quickly. "I'd be delighted," she replied. Her forehead wrinkled into a worried look, "But, will I need a fancy dress?"

"It is fairly formal and perhaps a bit stuffy; at the home of one of our professors. But I could possibly make some arrangement to assist you with a sort of shopping trip downtown."

"Doesn't that sound exciting, Tommy?"

"Could we all go to the party?"

"Good idea, Tommy. You already know Doctor Dugas."

"Will I get to see him there?"

"No doubt."

John had a fevered air about him and he had completely lost his concern of judgment by others.

"I had a close call with my accident. During your voyage across the Atlantic, you both must have experienced that sense, too. We have many things for which to be grateful. I'm going to say good night now, but I'll be back tomorrow evening with more details about the event. Thank you ever so much for the tea and soda bread."

Tommy interjected, "John, come for supper tomorrow night. We always eat at eight o'clock, after we get off from work."

John looked at Erin.

"Yes, that would be lovely. We eat dinner mid-day in the mill, so we have a light supper at day's end and we'd be delighted to have you join us." Erin had to catch her breath. She thought it was too good to be true, but now and with certainty, she believed it was better to wait for best.

"Alright, then. I will be here."

John fairly floated back to Mrs. Gardner's boarding house. He was happy he'd asked Erin and she'd said yes. Plus, he loved working with Tommy. He was such a bright boy, and John was inspired by his resilient spirit.

He made a grand entrance through the front door. "Hello, is anybody home?"

Gracie came running out from the dining room. "Mister John, is that you? Where has you been?"

"Oh, it's a long story, Gracie. I sort of fell in a hole and couldn't get out. Spent the whole night there."

"I sure is happy to see you. Miss Amanda and Broom will be, too."

"Where is Mrs. Gardner?"

Amanda came down the stairs. She had composed herself, fixed her hair, powdered her cheeks and begun her new medication.

"I'm right here. What happened to your arm?"

"It's a slight fracture, nothing serious. I'll be fine soon enough."

"Glad to hear that. Owen and Sterling are upstairs studying."

"Ain't you about starving, Mister John?"

"Actually, no, I've just had some tea and bread."

"Where did you stop off to get that?" Amanda remembered Owen's remark about a woman John might be seeing.

"I was at a new friend's house. Yet, another long story that I will tell, but not tonight. I was wondering, though, if you'd be willing to accompany a pretty young lady on a shopping trip to pick out a dress for the holiday social?"

"I would be delighted."

"That's settled then. Gracie, I do seem to have an appetite for a plate of your food. After which, a good night's sleep in my own bed is what this doctor in training is ordering."

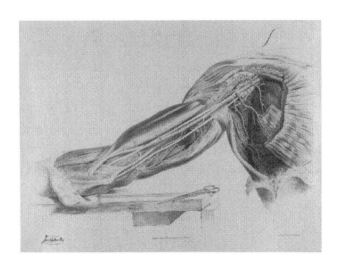

Chapter 31

Another Set Up

Setting up the dissecting room for the day's activities with three more bodies, Grandison was still worried and tired. He'd stayed up all night after putting Jacob Brown back in his Cedar Grove plot, sorting through all the confusing details of the previous day. His head was clear. There weren't any evil spirits. It had all been a case of mistaken identity. He'd even resolved the thought that he'd seen a ghost walking down the street, realizing that it must have been a look-a-like relative. Now, the only remaining, missing puzzle piece was John's whereabouts. He fretted about that.

The students began to arrive and take their places in the anatomy lab, including one John Wilkinson, Jr. with his left arm in its white cotton sling and signs of bruising underneath his right eye with black and blue mottling.

Owen passed by and leaned in to say, "Please make sure I'm in attendance when you tell the whole story. I really want to know what happened to you and I don't want to miss a word!"

Doctor Campbell remarked, "Nice to see you among the living Mr. Wilkinson. And what in the world happened to you?"

"Well, Professor Campbell, I was feeling quite poorly day before yesterday; extraordinarily weak and feeble. I fell down into a large hole and had some difficulty getting out. It seems as though I fractured my arm."

"It looks to be splinted well. We should expect your full recovery, then?"

"I'm counting on it."

Grandison Harris stared at John from across the room consciously clenching his teeth to keep his mouth from dropping. He'd never been so happy to see a live body before. He wanted to hug John, but instead he maintained his decorum and stood motionless, except for a bit of a grin that he couldn't control.

John gazed in Harris' direction and gave a wink. Then he chuckled, "During my confinement I seem to have gained a new appreciation for our cadavers' contributions to our anatomical discoveries and I must say that I feel most fortunate to be able to participate in today's lesson."

"Let us get on with it then," proclaimed Doctor Campbell.

Chapter 32

A Holiday Soiree

Broom maneuvered the horse and carriage around the muddy ruts in the road, leftovers from the afternoon winter rainstorm that was ushering in chillier weather. John sat in the back, giving directions.

"Turn left at the next corner and then right."

"Yes, sir, I knows the way to the mill, but I'll need you to point out the house when we gets close."

"Right . . . I guess I'm just a little nervous, Broom."

"What about, Mister John?"

"We're going round to pick up the most beautiful woman I know and I want this evening to go well."

"No reason to think it won't, is there?"

"No, I suspect not."

"Miss Amanda sure was happy when I takes her and Mr. Owen over to the party."

"Well, I just want to hurry up and get there." He bobbed his head around to get his bearings. "Next right,

Broom."

"Yes, sir."

"Alright, now it's the third house from the corner on the left." John could barely wait for Broom to stop the carriage as he leapt out and ran up the walkway.

Tommy, who'd been anxiously waiting by the front door, swung it open when he saw the carriage approach.

"John, do you like my new suit? I bought it myself at the company store with my own money. It's supposed to be a churchgoing outfit, but I figured it could go to a party, too." Tommy was sporting a black suit with matching waistcoat and bow-knotted cravat.

"Quite a handsome young man you are, Tommy, my boy."

"How's your arm, John?"

"It's almost good as new."

"Look, Auntie made me this special glove." Erin had fashioned her own special pattern for his left hand by knitting straight across between the first and pinky fingers, eliminating his two missing fingers' slots.

"That's perfect, isn't it?"

Erin Marie had been watching their interaction from the hallway. When John looked up and saw her, his mouth fell open. "Speaking of perfection . . . you look stunning, my dear." Erin was bedecked in her favorite color, a green velvet dress with tight bodice and cinched waist leading to a full hoop skirt. Amanda had insisted that Erin be fitted for the newest fashion craze of wire hoops, which she indulged herself in as well. Erin Marie's red hair was curled in tight ringlets all around her head. She was breathtaking.

"And both my young men look stunning as well." She smoothed her hands down the front skirt of her dress.

"May I take the liberty?" John pulled a jeweled necklace from his coat pocket. "My father gave this to me when I left home. He told me to save it for a special lady. You see … it belonged to my mother."

He clasped the necklace at the back of her neck. "I admit that I pressured Amanda to divulge the color of your outfit. When she said green, I was elated."

The emerald adornment sparkled. Erin felt the gems and held her hand flat against them as she went to the looking glass. She gasped, "I've never seen anything so beautiful."

"Shall we go? Our carriage awaits."

• • •

The house in the six hundred block of Greene Street was decorated with evergreen garlands and holly berries. A two-story attic frame built on a high brick basement; the home had been constructed in 1814. Double chimneys on both sides spewed their smoke and a wreath embellished the front door. An ornate wrought iron railing enclosed a porch and shutters paralleled the street-facing windows. The house was where Dean Newton resided.

Greeting guests at the door was the manservant for the evening, none other than Grandison Harris.

"Mr. Sterling, won't you come in with your lady friend, please."

"Thank you, Grandison. How are you this evening?"

"Very well, sir, thank you for asking."

They breezed into the foyer where Doctor Newton was greeting guests.

"Mr. Adams, how nice to see you."

"And you, too, Doctor Newton. Sir, may I present Miss Lucy Clark?"

Newton reached out his hand and took Lucy's as she gave a slight curtsey. "Charmed, I assure you."

Lucy was wearing a deep blue velvet dress with white

trimmed sleeves and collar. A matching bonnet tied under her chin completed her outfit. Sterling folded her hand into the crook of his elbow as they moved into the parlor. He noticed Amanda Gardner's red clad arm demurely waving from the corner of the room. Pushing gently past the throng of other students and holding Lucy's hand behind him in single file, he led their way in that direction.

"Lucy, let me introduce you to our landlady, Mrs. Gardner. This is Miss Lucy Clark."

"Why, Mrs. Gardner, I've heard ever so much about you and the comfortable home you provide for Sterling and his colleagues."

"Let me leave you two lovely ladies to chat for a few moments."

Sterling had found Owen amidst the guests. "Did you see who greeted us at the front door?"

"Yes, Grandison Harris. He is certainly a man of many talents. I heard mention that he serves at many of these types of functions."

"Man of many talents . . . right. How is it with Amanda?"

"Things seem fine, now. I do believe she has come to an understanding that the nature of our relationship is strictly friendship. And in that light, I was pleased to escort her tonight."

A slight hush came over the room as John entered the parlor accompanying Erin Marie and Tommy. A buzz of conversation quickly followed as the regulars of the social scene discussed the identity of the newcomers.

The trio flowed into the dining room, where a spread of food adorned the table and a group of string musicians played Mozart in the far corner.

"What kind of food is that? Little bits and pieces on those plates?" Tommy started to point at the plates, but

John pushed his arm down.

"They are called hors d'oeuvres. Served at parties like this, it's a dainty sort of food. You eat it gently with your fingers, like so." John gingerly picked up a stuffed mushroom and gracefully showed Tommy the procedure. "Now, you."

Tommy mimicked John's moves.

"Quite, nice, young man."

"And they taste good, too. Try one, Auntie."

Tommy caught sight of Doctor Dugas who was walking toward them.

The physician shook hands with John, and then turned to Erin. "Miss McLennan, so nice to see you this evening." He turned his gaze to Tommy. "And young man, your studies, how are they progressing?"

"I've begun to work on my second reading primer."

John put his arm around Tommy's shoulders. "I'm so proud of him. I told Tommy I'd be bringing him journal articles soon."

"Excellent, we certainly have need of enthusiastic learners with dedicated mentors in this medical profession of ours. So nice to see you and please excuse me as I make my rounds."

John reached out and put his other arm around Erin. "I'm so glad you both came with me tonight."

Erin smiled, "And we three are picnicking with Maureen tomorrow?"

"Yes, certainly. I'm looking forward to meeting her."

Tommy tugged at John's sleeve, "John, I really will be a doctor someday, won't I?"

"Yes indeed, Tommy, and so will I."

Postscript

As a tradition, all good medical students pass along their best stories. Several versions of the prank played on Grandison Harris that late autumn night so long ago have been passed down. Here are two of them:

One night Grandison (who was in the midst of a job) stopped in an alley behind a saloon and went inside to refresh himself. Two medical students who had been watching him removed the body from Harris' sack, hid it and one of them got in the sack. When Grandison returned to his wagon, one student groaned in a grave-like voice: Grandison... Grandison... I'm cold. Buy me a drink!

Before running away, Harris supposedly said, "You buy your own drink 'cause I'm getting out of here!"

Augusta Chronicle, 1995

On a typical evening while Grandison was imbibing, the students substituted one of their own number for the corpse, having already posted watchers along the remainder of the route to note Grandison's reaction at the climactic moment of their scheme. The powerful Negro made his exit from the bar, shouldered his load, and proceeded on his journey as usual. As he was walking along the 300 block of Walker Street, a deep and mournful voice from within the sack broke the deep silence of the evening, "Grandison, what is you gwine do wit me?"

According to the witnesses, Grandison stopped dead in his tracks and without a moment's hesitation exclaimed in a loud but quivering voice, "I'se gwine drap you rat now."

This he did, disappearing quickly, and for three days afterwards Grandison was not seen at the College.

SJ Lewis,
Chronicle of an Institution,
part 1, page 155

Notes on Grandison Harris

Grandison Harris' career with the Medical College of Georgia began in 1852 when he was purchased for seven hundred dollars for the purpose of procuring subjects for anatomical study. He was reunited with his wife and son when the Medical College purchased both of them in 1858. Beginning as a slave with a period of interruption during the Civil War and Reconstruction, he returned as a full-time employee with a salary of eight dollars per month. Besides his duties as porter, he also served at social functions and parties for the faculty. He was promoted to janitor in 1895.

Besides providing the college with subjects for dissection and performing his janitorial duties, he learned to read and write and became quite knowledgeable in the subject of anatomy. He was known to assist students and some even thought he held an honorary Doctoral degree from the school. Harris read obituary notices to plan his schedule of corpse capture. He was reportedly so skilled at removing bodies and making the gravesites look undisturbed, although there were suspicions, he maintained his secrets for many years.

Harris was loved and respected. He became a member of the Pythians Masonic Lodge, a group that, for some, represented a symbol of success in black middle-class society. He was viewed as having a leadership role among his peers and was respected for his position and power. He gave elaborate parties for the VIPs in the black community in the manner and style he became accustomed to while serving the medical college faculty.

Harris was also loathed and feared. Because it was unclear exactly how he had gained the favoritism of the faculty at the college or what he did to earn the money that allowed him to maintain an extraordinary lifestyle, a shroud of mystery surrounded him and his activities.

Toward the last decade of the nineteenth century, as suspicions grew regarding Harris' activities, the indignation centered on whose relatives might have been victim to his shovel.

He was said to be a dazzling dresser, donning black suits in winter and sporting a derby hat, then switching to all white suits in summer topped with a white Panama straw hat. In his lapel he wore a boutonniere, most often a red rose.

He died in 1911 and, ironically, was buried in Cedar Grove Cemetery. His actual gravesite remains a mystery because the cemetery records were lost in a flood in 1929.

Harris may be seen by some as a betrayer of his culture for providing the cadavers of his kinsmen. However, studying the dead was perceived as the only way to truly advance the practice of medicine at that time. And although he defiled the graves viewed as sacred final resting-places for those departed, their "forced" donation and cumulative contribution to the body of knowledge called Modern Medicine cannot be overstated.

Epilogue

Details surrounding the bodies taken over the course of years from the Cedar Grove Cemetery might never have been known to the extent that it is today, if the bones in the basement of the old Medical College hadn't been discovered in 1989. While excavating to prepare for renovation, human bones were discovered. Fearing the unearthing of a mass murderer's trove, calls went from Augusta to Atlanta's State Crime Lab and eventually resulted in an archeological study by Robert Blakely and students at Georgia State University. Medical artifacts were abundant. Thousands of skeletal parts were found. They were concluded to be left over from dissections performed at the college for purpose of instructing medical students. Most of the bones had been layered in lime and were well preserved. Estimated individuals numbered between five hundred-ninety and six hundred-ten.

The subsequent scientific analysis yielded much information about the practice of medicine in the nineteenth and early twentieth century and findings were published in a book entitled *Bones in the Basement* in 1997.

All the bones were returned to the Medical College in 1998 and re-interred in a sealed vault in Cedar Grove Cemetery, located at 120 Watkins Street in Augusta, Georgia. The headstone's inscription reads:

Known But to God

May the remains of these souls find perpetual peace in
this, their final resting place.
We grieve that these human beings were disturbed
from their original resting places,
Yet we celebrate their lasting gift to mankind.
In the 1800s and early 1900s at
the Medical College of Georgia,
physicians and physicians-in-training
studied these remains, God's handiwork,
to glean new information about the human body.
Following their discovery in 1990 at
the Old Medical College of Georgia
on Telfair Street, the remains provided insight
into the medical practices and health of the 19th century.
Immeasurable medical, scientific and
anthropological knowledge about an urban
population that lived during the Civil War and
Reconstruction has been preserved
for future generations.
This is a loving testament and tribute
to their unknowing heroism and altruism.

May they Rest in Eternal Peace
November 7, 1998

...And then the digging was done.

Other Anecdotal Notes

Burke, Hare, Laird, McDougal and Doctor Knox

Following William Burke's hanging on January 28, 1829, his three comrades searched for obscurity. Helen McDougal was found by an angry mob after her release and had to be escorted to safety by police. She left Scotland for England and is said to have died in Australia in 1868.

Margaret Hare also had to be rescued several times by police for her own security due to attack whenever she was recognized. She was last seen boarding a steamboat bound for Belfast, Ireland.

William Hare was released from jail in early February 1829, but was a continual victim of inadequate disguise. It is rumored that he roamed the streets of London, a blind beggar, as a result of being thrown into a lime pit by avenging townsfolk. His last documented sighting was in the English town of Carlisle.

Doctor Knox continued giving lectures and classes in Edinburgh, but by 1836, the numbers of students interested in his lectures dwindled. Although he reportedly maintained silence about his associations with Burke and Hare, his house and classroom was occasionally stormed by an angry mob. He promoted his 1846 book, The Races of Men, which explained his theories of ethnic inferiorities. He moved to London and held a post at the Cancer Hospital until he died in 1862. Plaster heads of Burke and Hare are kept in the museums at the Royal College of Surgeons of Edinburgh and the University of Edinburgh. Burke's skeleton remains in the Anatomy Museum at Edinburgh University.

Yellow Fever

A Cuban physician, Carlos Finlay, theorized in 1881 that the causative agent of yellow fever was the Aedes aegypti mosquito. Walter Reed, a United States Army physician and head of the Yellow Fever Commission, was sent to Cuba to devise human experiments to test Finlay's theory. Members of the commission, soldiers of the occupying force, and civilian employees volunteered as subjects. In 1901, the commission reported that the mosquito was an intermediate host of the disease. They proved that yellow fever was transmitted only through the mosquito's bite and not by direct contact between infected persons.

Eradication of mosquito breeding grounds has seriously diminished Yellow Fever. Protective clothing, screens, mosquito netting and repellents are all preventative agents, and a vaccine is available in areas where there is a high prevalence of the disease. According to the Center for Disease Control and Prevention (CDC), the disease currently occurs in sub-Saharan Africa and tropical South America.

The Augusta Canal

Complaints by factory owners regarding the amount of power the canal could sustain led to an analysis that found it to be inadequate for its intended purpose. Miscalculations on the number of spindles that could be powered by the water on the canal proved expensive. At a total cost of over $900,000, the canal enlargement project from 1871-1875 did bring remedy to the power problem. The industrial growth of Henry H. Cumming's vision took place, but he did not live to see it. He committed suicide on April 14, 1866. He was said to have incurred heavy expenses during the Civil War and he was affected by the "troubles of our suffering country."

William Phillips, the man who devoted his professional career to the care and maintenance of the canal, lost his wife to it when she was thirty-eight. It was believed she drowned while walking along its banks. He was removed from his positions as Canal and Waterworks Engineer in 1869; however, he continued his close association with the canal by making a map in 1875 displaying all its factories and features.

The Augusta canal continues to operate. It was dedicated as a National Heritage area in 1996. Tours are available on replica cargo boats as well as recreational opportunities on the towpath, trail and waterway. An interpretive center at the Enterprise Mill displays its history.

Anesthesia

Controversy has surrounded the discovery of anesthesia. The first public demonstration of ether in 1846 occurred in Boston and was delivered before Harvard medical students by William Thomas Green Morton, a dentist. A well-known surgeon, John C. Warren, had agreed to allow Morton to administer ether to his patient as Warren performed surgical removal of a neck tumor. A colleague of Morton's, Horace Wells, had attempted a demonstration using nitrous oxide two years earlier, but the patient cried out when his tooth was extracted and the exercise was declared a failure.

After Morton's success, he saw opportunity for financial gain and attempted to patent ether, trying to disguise it and rename it Letheon. The ruse was unsuccessful and within months ether was being employed in both the United States and Europe, negating the patent application.

Wells became addicted to chloroform and committed suicide in jail in 1848 at the age of thirty-three, but the American Dental Association credited him with the discovery of practical anesthesia and its introduction to the U.S. in 1864.

Morton died at the age of forty-nine in 1868 after twenty years of litigation and poverty. His family was left with no money.

Crawford Long came forward and announced his 1844 ether experiments to the students and faculty at MCG in 1848. His delay in disclosure has been explained by the suspension of the *Southern Medical and Surgical Journal* from 1839-1845, and by the fact that Doctors Paul Eve and Alexander Dugas were embroiled in their own controversy between anesthesia and mesmerism. Today he is widely recognized as being the first to use anesthesia in a surgical operation.

Ireland

Combined forces of famine, disease and emigration depopulated Ireland from eight million to five million between 1846 and 1850. As many as a million lives were lost to the potato blight and subsequent epidemics of cholera and typhus. Many Irish blamed centuries of British political oppression for their plight. As English landlords raised their rents, Irish tenant farmers were being evicted for non-payment. Some landlords paid for their tenants to emigrate and the famine spurred waves of immigration to the United States.

Cholera

Cholera, an acute infection of the gastrointestinal tract,

is caused by Vibrio cholerae, a gram-negative flagellum. Characterized by extreme dehydration in its most severe cases, it causes shock and acidosis resulting from rapid loss of fluids and electrolytes. Untreated, death may occur rapidly, in as little as two to twelve hours after the onset of diarrhea. It occurs in situations with inadequate sanitation and nutrition. Three major North American epidemics occurred in 1832, 1848 and in 1867.

During the twentieth century, cholera was confined mostly to Asia. With the advent of intravenous fluids, treatment has been highly successful and survival rates indicate that today's prognosis is excellent. In 1991 a cholera epidemic spread in South America. According to the CDC, it is still common in certain parts of the world, including the Indian subcontinent and sub-Saharan Africa.

Addiction

Humans have sought to alter consciousness throughout the ages, but in the 1800s it reached a fever pitch. Laudanum, a tincture of opium dissolved in alcohol, was wildly popular. Cheaper than gin, it became a drug of the working class. Doctors prescribed it for almost every ailment. It became the drug of choice by some of the romantic poets, Lord Byron, Percy Shelley, John Keats, Sara Coleridge and Elizabeth Barrett Browning, to name a few. Opium extracts and alcohol were also main ingredients in hosts of over-the-counter medicines with names like Dover's powder, Godfrey's Cordial, Dr. J. Collis Browne's Chlorodyne, Mrs. Winslow's Soothing Syrup, and Wistar's Balsam of Wild Cherry.

Not thought to be addictive, morphine became a popular substance by the mid 1850's. During the Civil War, following the invention of the hypodermic needle, its use as a pain-relieving agent created thousands of addicts.

In 1874, a new drug named heroin was hailed as safe, non-addictive and a substitute for morphine.

The Harrison Narcotics Act of 1914 was designed to control medicinal opium, morphine, heroin and cocaine. It required pharmacists and doctors to register with the Treasury Department, pay taxes and keep records of narcotics prescribed or dispensed.

Child Labor Laws in the State of Georgia

Child labor laws were enacted beginning on September 1, 1906. It prohibited the employment in any factory or manufacturing establishment of children less than ten years of age under any circumstances. The following January, the law extended to children under the age of twelve unless they were an orphan with no other means of support or had a widowed mother or disabled father dependent on their earnings.

Night work between the hours of seven in the evening and six in the morning was prohibited for children under fourteen on January 1, 1908. These same children were required to be able to read and write and receive twelve weeks of schooling, with at least six weeks of it to occur consecutively.

Anatomical Act

Effective in June 1834, a law was enacted to define the illegal acquisition of cadavers. It included any person or persons who removed the dead body of a human being from a grave or other place of interment or from any vault, tomb, sepulcher or from any place, without the consent of the friends of said deceased. An exception existed for dissections of executed criminals.

The law was neither followed nor enforced, primarily due to medical schools' specimen requirement for the demonstration of anatomy lessons.

In 1887, the law was revised when the Georgia Legislature passed an act designed to protect cemeteries and burying places. A board of overseers was created to supervise the distribution and use of unclaimed bodies from prison, chain gangs, penitentiaries, morgues and public hospitals in the state. For the promotion of medical science, the board added a provision to ensure that bodies would be distributed to colleges. This was to ensure that they would no longer be put in the position of having to rob graves to obtain their subjects.

Selected Bibliography

Adams, N. (2002). *Scottish Bodysnatchers*. Goblinshead. Musselburgh.

Allen, L. (1976). Grandison Harris, Sr.: Slave, Resurrectionist and Judge. *Bulletin of the Georgia Academy of Science* 34:192-199.

Augusta Canal. *History of the Augusta Canal*. Retrieved from http://www.augustacanal.com

Augusta Chronicle. Slave Had Vital Role for MCG. Retrieved from http://www.augustachronicle.com (Original article published in the *Augusta Chronicle* August, 1995.)

Blakely, R.L & Harrington, J.M. (Eds.). (1997). *Bones in the Basement*. Washington, DC: Smithsonian Institute.

Burton, O.V. (1985). *In My Father's House are Many Mansions - Family and Community in Edgefield, South Carolina*. Chapel Hill: University of North Carolina Press.

Cashin, E.J. (2002). *The Brightest Arm of the Savannah*. Augusta: Augusta Canal Authority.

Cashin, E.J. (1996). *The Story of Augusta*. Richmond County Historical Society. Spartanburg: The Reprint Co.

Chandler, J.D. (1991, April). The Old Medical College: A Living Monument to History and Medicine. *Journal of MAG*. Vol. 80. 213-218.

De Kruif, P. (1940). *Microbe Hunters*. New York: Pocket Books.

Eidson, S. (2001, January 11-17). Augusta's Living Dead. *The Metropolitan Spirit*. Augusta, GA. Pg. 13-15.

Ellison, L. (2002, May 30). **Southern Medical and Surgical Journal** A Chronicle of Medical Discovery. *Moments in MCG History*. Retrieved from http://www.mcg.edu/history/mcgmoments.asp

Ellison, L. (2002, June 27). Mesmerism, hypnosis: Campus connections from 1845-2002. *Moments in MCG History*. Retrieved from http://www.mcg.edu/history/mcgmoments.asp

Ellison, L. (2002, March 21). The MCG Connection to Dr. Crawford W. Long's Discovery of Ether. *Moments in MCG History*. Retrieved from http://www.mcg.edu/history/mcgmoments.asp

Goodrich, W.H. (1928). *The History of the Medical Department of the University of Georgia*. Augusta: Ridgely-Tilwell.

Gregg, W. (1845). *Essays on domestic industry: or, An enquiry into the expediency of establishing cotton manufactures in South Carolina*. Charleston: Burges & James. Rare Book Collection at the Wilson Library. University of North Carolina. Chapel Hill, NC.

Hodgson, B. (2001). *In the Arms of Morpheus*. Buffalo: Firefly Books.

Hunter, G.W., Frye, W.W., Swartzwelder, J.C. (1966). *A Manual of Tropical Medicine*. 4th Edition. Philadelphia: W. B. Saunders.

Hunter, S. (Web-posted 1996, June 21). 'Resurrection Man' dug way into history. *Augusta Chronicle*. Retrieved from http://www.augustachronicle.com

Lewis, S.J. (1963). *The Medical College of Georgia 1829-1963 Chronicle of an Institution.* Vol.1. Bound Thesis, Robert B Greenblatt, MD Library. Medical College of Georgia. Augusta, GA.

Lyons, A.S. & Petrucelli, R.J. (1987). *Medicine: An Illustrated History.* New York: Abradale Press. Harry N. Abrams, Inc.

Medical College of Georgia History – 175 years of Teaching, Discovering and Caring. Retrieved from http://www.mcg.edu/library/history

Moores, R.R. (1976, January-March). MCG Yesterday. *Intercom.* (Vol. 6, Nos. 1-6). Historical Collections and Archives. Robert B. Greenblatt, M.D. Library. Medical College of Georgia. Augusta, GA.

Richardson, R. (1987). *Death, dissection and the destitute.* New York: Routledge & Kegan Paul.

Roach, M. (2003). *STIFF - The Curious Lives of Human Cadavers.* New York: W.H. Norton.

Royland, A.R., Callahan, H. (1976). *Yesterday's Augusta.* Miami: E A Seemann Publishing.

Southern Medical and Surgical Journal. (1836-1838). (Vols. 1-2). & (1845-1854). (Vols. 1-10). [various articles]. Historical Collections and Archives. Robert B. Greenblatt, M.D. Library. Medical College of Georgia. Augusta, GA.

Spalding, P. (1987). *The History of the Medical College of Georgia.* Athens: University of Georgia Press.

Stevenson, R.L. (1998). *The Body Snatcher.* Adapted by Kulling, M. New York: Random House.

52552175R00143

Made in the USA
Columbia, SC
10 March 2019